Colours of Magic

Anna Novak

*To my parents,
my sister Karolina
and my partner Michal
with love, J.R.*

Prologue

It's incredible how one person can change your life. You never know what's awaiting around the corner, what destiny has prepared for you or where your fate will take you. And what if you had a chance to live forever? Would you hesitate with an answer?

Chapter 1

Hayley was sitting on a couch with a cup of hot coffee, staring at the TV without even knowing what she was watching. Her green eyes were no longer watery and red but there was no life reflecting in them either. She was numb, switched off. Life hasn't been the same since her husband died last year in a car accident. They used to spend every minute together. Life was full of laughter and adventures, it was never boring and now it's just eat - work - sleep - repeat. Hayley had a feeling that she would never be happy again and yet, she didn't feel ready to die. *'Time heals all wounds.'* she kept telling herself and waited patiently for her life to change. The only people visiting her were her younger sisters June and April, twins who she loved very much but they were never her best friends.

- You need to get out, have some fun – said June once - There are wonderful things out there waiting for you. Art, music, amazing people, breathtaking views. You can't keep living like this Hayley, you don't want to spend the rest of your life alone, stuck in this house.

Hayley wanted to go out and enjoy her life but she didn't want to experience all that alone. And yet, she was not looking for anyone, her work was taking much of her time anyway. Hayley was a psychologist and she liked helping people. Her husband was a psychiatrist and he loved the mystery of a human brain, it fascinated him. Hayley, on the other hand, was terrified how mental illness could take control of a human body. That's why she decided psychology would be enough and she didn't have to dive any deeper into one's mind. Now, however, she needed to dive into hers to search for a remedy for her sadness and loneliness. She remembered how some of her patients changed when they got themselves a pet. She never actually thought about having a pet, she liked having her house clean and pets would make a mess. She also liked making last-minute reservations and popping out somewhere with her husband and there was nobody to take care of a pet then. But now, she didn't plan on going anywhere, she was not interested in travelling alone and her sisters would make terrible companions.

'*Let's get a dog*' the unexpected thought filled her heart with joy. She put the empty mug down, turned the TV off and reached for her laptop. As she started browsing the internet, she realised how many puppies were looking for their forever home. She wanted a loyal dog, a protective one, a dog that would make her feel safe. And so she decided to get a German Shephard. She didn't have to browse for too long having found a perfect match within ten minutes. The puppy has been advertised for a month. Apparently, the owner died and there was nobody to take care of the puppy now. It was already five months old therefore harder to sell. The puppy was over a hundred miles away but Hayley wanted to take a road trip. She felt for that poor, lonely creature that nobody wanted. '*Looks like we both lost someone and ended up alone*' she thought. Without much more thinking she dialled the number.

- Hi, I'm calling regarding the puppy that you advertised. Is it still available?

- Hi, yes, she's still here - the lady on the phone sounded relieved and happy - Good you called because I was about to take her to the shelter tomorrow.

- Sounds like it was just meant to be. I will pop in tomorrow afternoon. I have a long drive ahead of me, I'm from Aspen.

- That is going to be a long drive indeed, I'm glad you decided to come anyway. I will text you my address now.

- Can you also text me the information about the food she's on? I don't want to upset her stomach with anything new.

- Of course, no problem. See you tomorrow.

Hayley hung up and sighed. Her heart was beating fast with excitement and anxiety. She knew it was going to be a huge change in her life, that the dog would give her some purpose and make her feel better. She closed her laptop, put her long brown hair into a messy ponytail, grabbed her wallet and car keys and went out shopping to have everything ready for the next day. Rocky Mountains Pet Shop had everything she needed. She didn't even have a list prepared, she was just walking from one aisle to another, taking all dog-related products. She left the store with a full trolley, hoping she didn't forget anything. Unpacking all that stuff at home made her even happier and she couldn't wait for that dog to arrive. She moved the food and water bowls from one place to another at least a few times, trying to find the right spot. She put all toys in one large basket in the corner of the living room and a large bone on the rug by the sofa, hoping it would attract dog's attention. Before she turned the lights off, she had a look around. The house already looked better with all the dog stuff lying around. She smiled and went upstairs but the feeling of anticipation couldn't let her fall asleep so she turned her laptop on and typed: *'How to train a puppy.'*

It was a long road trip to Colorado Springs but Hayley enjoyed it. She felt so free and wild when she was driving on a highway in her red two thousand seventeen Ford Mustang GT. She loved her car and driving it was a pure pleasure. Her and her husband put all their savings into that car when they decided not to throw a big expensive wedding and have a small ceremony instead. That car took them to many beautiful places and was a witness of countless conversations, laughter and tears so Hayley was taking a good care of it, making sure it would last forever.

She was driving fast and singing out loud knowing that nobody could hear her. She didn't think of herself as a good singer but she didn't care. She was by herself, free to sing whatever she wanted. Every time she was singing along, she remembered that scene from the Scary Movie 2 where Cindy was driving and singing and the lady on the radio asked her to shut up. That always made Hayley smile. She enjoyed a good comedy, she had a good sense of humour and everyone she knew considered her funny. She didn't watch any horror movies or dramas as she thought that life was terrifying and sad enough as it was. The stories told by her patients made her realise how terrible life could get sometimes and she was grateful that her life wasn't that bad. And it was about to get even better now. She couldn't wait to meet the puppy. What a change it would be in her boring, sad and monotonous life. A dog would definitely be unpredictable and out of control at first. It would force Hayley to go out despite the weather or her mood. It would always be there to cheer her up and make her laugh or get on her nerves and make her angry. *'I know it's a good decision.* - she thought - *A puppy will keep my mind busy. I have so much free time so I can spend it on training it. It's going to be fun, I'm sure of it.'* Hayley took a deep breath and glanced at the mountains around. All road seventy was nothing but open spaces, wild mountains and hills either overgrown with trees and short bushes or sharp and hard as a rock. She loved Colorado for its wilderness and she couldn't picture herself living anyplace else. As a new track started in her player, Hayley turned it up with a smile and started to sing again: *'Fast on a rough road riding, high through the mountains climbing, twisting, turning further from my home...'*

By the time she reached her destination, she had a hoarse voice and a sore throat. She got out of her car and started walking towards the house. It was big, stylish, quite new and situated just outside the city. There were two Dobermanns in the garden that started to bark when they saw Hayley at the gate. The front door opened before Hayley rang the gate bell.

- Hi, you must be Hayley. I'm Alicia. Please, come in. Your puppy is inside and ready to go.

She promptly locked the dogs in the kennel and let Hayley in. The house looked very impressive. Alicia must have been rich or having a loan for the rest of her life. Either way, the house looked expensive. Alicia was a stylish lady in her fifties. There was not a single grey hair on her head, her nails were nicely done and her clothes looked expensive. *'What a classy lady'* Hayley thought.

- I like your place. It's a very nice house.

- Thank you. We built it two years ago. I moved here with my husband after our kids moved out. We decided to sell our apartment in the city and grow old here.

- It was definitely a good decision. The place looks very lovely.

- Thank you. So, Hayley, this is the pappy.

Hayley looked at a big dog lying on the rug in the living room. Typical German Shepherd – black and brown with short coat and big pointy ears. The dog looked at them with interest but didn't get up.

- I don't know her name and we didn't come up with anything. She was my friend's dog. She's very cute but we cannot keep her as unfortunately, my other two dogs don't like her very much and she's afraid of them. I kept her inside the house for those past few weeks but she requires a constant attention and a proper training. Are you sure you're ready for this?

- No problem, I work from home so she won't be alone too much. I can also take a few weeks off and focus on her completely.

- Sounds great. I have a collar, harness, leash and some dry food. I also have a dog bed that you can take. Maybe she will be less afraid if she has some familiar smell in her new home.

- Thank you Alicia. Let me take this all to my car and I will come back for her.

Hayley was very excited but also terrified. It has just hit her, all of a sudden, that it was a living creature that would need her every day and require her constant attention. She knew that of course but it all became so real when she saw the dog. *'I can do it. It's not a baby, it's just a dog. It can't be too difficult'* she thought. When she turned around Alicia was already walking towards her with the dog on a leash. They both got the dog on the back seat and put the seatbelt on by clipping it to the harness.

- Looks like you're both good to go now. Good luck and let me know if you have any more questions.

- Thanks Alicia, it was nice meeting you. Take care.

Hayley turned the Sat Nav on and started driving back home.

- Hi little girl. – she said looking at the dog's reflection in the mirror - I hope you're comfortable back there because there is a long drive ahead of us. I hope you don't mind me singing because I plan on signing all the way back home. I promise I will think of a right name for you.

But instead of singing, Hayley ended up talking to the puppy. She talked about her work and her sisters and her husband. She also described the house and the garden and the park nearby. The dog sat quietly the whole journey, either looking through the window or sleeping. Before Heyley even realised, they were already in Aspen.

- You are an excellent listener. I already like you.

Hayley parked her car on the driveway and looked at the dog over her shoulder.

- So what should I call you? Nala? ... Lola? ... Lexi? Lexi sounds good, don't you think?

She opened the door and let the dog in. Lexi stopped at the door and sniffed.

- Come on, girl, it's your home now.

Hayley walked in first trying to encourage the dog to follow. Lexi took a few steps and sat down.

- You want to sit here? That's fine, no pressure. Whenever you're ready.

Hayley went to the kitchen and made a cup of coffee for herself and prepared a bowl of wet wood for Lexi. She put the bowl on a floor by the fridge, sat down at the table and waited. After a couple of minutes, she saw Lexi slowly approaching the bowl. The dog ate its content rapidly and looked at Hayley hoping there would be more to come.

- No, I won't give you more food for another three hours. But you can have a treat if you want.

Hayley reached to her. Lexi approached her slowly and ate the food off Hayley's hand, wagging its tail.

- I think we're going to be just fine – she added with a smile and petted the dog. – You want to see the garden? Come on!

And so Lexi became the centre of Hayley's life. She was talking to her, taking trips with her, watching movies, crying and laughing with Lexi by her side. Getting that pet was her first step in getting better. And she got better. She got herself a purpose, a responsibility and most of all, she didn't feel lonely anymore.

Chapter 2

Liam was sitting in an armchair with a book in one hand and a glass of bourbon in the other. It was a Monday morning and not a good time for early drinking but he had absolutely nothing better to do. His black hair was messy and the sweats he was wearing should already be in the laundry basket. He didn't have to go anywhere, nobody needed him, nobody waited for him and he had no responsibilities or whatsoever. It was a morning like any other and he knew his sister Isabella would come over and check up on him any time soon. She always did that. He knew she cared about him deeply and he loved her very much too but he was tired of being treated like a little boy who needed to be looked after.

He was about to put the book down when the door opened and his sister came in.

- Hi brother, how was your weekend?

She asked that question although she already knew the answer. Monday morning and Liam was already drinking, sitting in his sweats. It was a sad view and it was breaking her heart that she didn't know how to help him. All she wanted was to see him smile again, to be happy, to live because he wanted to and not because he must. She visited him as often as she could, hoping his life would change eventually but every time she appeared in that door, she saw the same view.

- At home, as usual, boring.

That was the answer she expected but didn't want to hear.

- I was thinking... Maybe we could go to Miami together? See our friends, have some fun, enjoy the ocean... What do you think?

Liam looked into Isabella's blue eyes. It was so clear she was troubled and sad.

- Good idea, I could use some time off.

Isabella watched Liam drinking his bourbon and looking pensive. She worried about him but didn't know how to ask the question.

- Liam... - she started still unsure whether it's a good idea to start that topic - you have been miserable for some time now and I have no idea why. Please, be honest with me for once and tell me, what's happened?

Liam didn't want to be honest with his sister. He wanted to be that strong, big brother she always looked up to. He didn't want to admit out loud that he was unhappy but he knew she would not stop asking.

- I feel lonely, Isabella. We keep changing houses but I am never home, we keep making new friends but we always abandon them, sooner or later. We build our lives for a few years and then we start all over again someplace else. I am happy I have you and I love you, but...

- Oh, I get it, we need to put you on the market again. I will set up an online profile for you and we'll find you someone in no time.

Liam sighed.

- I don't want girls from the internet, they're shallow and they don't care about anything or anyone other than themselves. They look for fun and excitement and I already had that. I want someone warm and gentle, someone good and compassionate. I'm done with short-term relationships leading to nowhere. I want someone to be with me for who I am... But I cannot be myself with anyone and I'm tired of pretending being someone else. I'm tired, Isabella.

She didn't know what to say. Liam surprised her with his honesty and she couldn't find any right words that would soothe his pain.

- Don't worry sister, I will get over it. It's just a short episode of my never-ending existence. Just give me some time and I will get back to my usual self, I'll be fine.

Liam hated feeling lonely. He had relationships that lasted for a couple of years but that was it. He liked his life as it was but the hardest part of it was loneliness. He was not looking for adventures, he wanted simple things - a dinner out, a long walk in the park, a quiet evening in front of a TV. But he wanted to share all those moments with someone. Life was difficult those days with social media and constant pressure to look better, to have more. Nobody was looking for love anymore, people wanted fun and excitement but not love. They were selecting their partners carefully, comparing them to others. What happened to real emotions and feelings? When has life become that constant race, that never-ending competition? Maybe Liam should accept the fact that love didn't exist anymore. Maybe he should stop searching for emotions that were long gone and start to live his life like the others. Maybe he should take that trip with Isabella and meet their friends in Miami. Liam liked the ocean and the beach, he was a good surfer and an excellent swimmer. A few days off sounded like a good idea and he needed to break the routine.

- Leave it with me – he said getting up from the armchair – I will book the tickets and the hotel and arrange everything. - he smiled gently, trying to look convincing.

Shortly after Isabella has left, Liam grabbed his helmet and went for a ride on his motorbike to clear his mind. Speeding down the highway always made him feel better as all troubles seemed to be left behind. He wanted a better life although he had everything that money could buy. He could make all his dreams come true very easily, doing whatever he wanted, buying whatever he wanted. But what hurt him the most was returning to an empty house and having all those wonderful moments and no one to share them with. A reach life spent alone was worth nothing and he learnt it the hard way. Liam was very likeable, smart and handsome but his darkest secrets always prevented him from having a meaningful relationship that would last forever. He hated the fact that he was forced to face the eternity surrounded by strangers who meant absolutely nothing and no matter how hard he tried, a true love was nowhere to be found.

Chapter 3

Lexi became Hayley's whole world and a centre of her existence. Whenever she didn't work, she spent time with the dog. Alicia was right saying that the puppy required a lot of attention. Lexi was out of control at first but she was a very smart dog and Hayley managed to train her well in just a few weeks. She needed her to listen and not to pull on the leash as she was a large and heavy dog and Hayley didn't want her to hurt anyone or any other animal. It was breaking her heart every time she was reaching for a muzzle. Lexi looked at her as if she was trying to say 'why are you doing this to me?' but Hayley couldn't risk any incidents and it was the only way to keep everyone around safe. But the more they went out, the more obedient Lexi was so after just two weeks, Hayley could throw the muzzle away and let Lexi off the leash to play with a stick or a ball. Hayley loved the new routine and all the responsibilities that came with Lexi. Getting that dog was the best decision she has made that year and the only regret she had was that she hasn't made that decision sooner.

It was dark, windy and cold - typical October evening and the forecast predicted snow. Hayley decided to go out for a walk without Lexi, it was going to be just a short walk around the neighbourhood that would help her quickly fall asleep. She didn't like being outside after sunset, without her dog. Lexi was very protective of her and made her feel safe, but in that moment, Hayley didn't feel like stopping every few seconds so Lexi could sniff every tree they passed by. She wanted a short, fast-paced walk and she knew the dog would just slow her down.

- Tonight, you're staying home, Lexi. You wouldn't like the weather outside anyway, trust me. I'll be right back.

Hayley put her jacket on, grabbed the scarf and the winter hat and left before Lexi could squeeze through the door. She walked quickly for a few minutes and then she started to jog. The streets were completely empty, the moon was covered with heavy clouds and the cold wind quickly frosted her face.

She was already on her way back home when she noticed someone at the end of the street, walking in her direction. *'He's just going to pass you by, don't worry'* she told herself. But there was something unusual about that guy and it terrified her. He looked normal in the darkness and there was no particular reason to be afraid but there was nobody else around and Hayley didn't like it. She stopped jogging and started walking instead. The man was approaching her, getting closer and closer. Hayley's every muscle tightened as she prepared herself to run or to fight. Suddenly, the man grabbed her by her arms and bit her neck. She felt extreme pain and even though she wanted to scream and run, she couldn't move, as if she was paralysed. There was no way to fight him back, she was completely defenceless. Tears came to her eyes and she thought she was going to die but all of a sudden, the attacker let her go as some other man pulled him away. Hayley couldn't believe her own eyes. She watched how that other man put his hand through the attacker's chest and ripped his heart out. Then, the heart and the rest of the body turned into ashes and disappeared in the air. The man looked at Hayley. He was tall and well-built and his blue eyes and dark hair nicely contrasted with his pale face. He didn't look scary but Hayley didn't want to take her chances and put her trust in a complete stranger.

- Let me help you. – he said. His voice was warm and calming.

But without much thinking, Hayley started running away as fast as she could. Not for too long though. She took only a few steps before she passed out.

Liam was in his kitchen preparing popcorn. It was going to be another boring evening in front of a TV, in a quiet, empty house that never felt like home. He was about to put the bag into the microwave when he saw some girl being attacked right outside his window. Without hesitation, he stormed outside, grabbed the guy and ripped his heart out. He's done it many times in the past and something as terrible as taking a life did not evoke any emotions or feelings in him. It was just another cruel and ruthless vampire who didn't deserve to live and Liam didn't care he had to kill him, it didn't bother him at all, even though it sounded horrible. He's done it to protect an innocent girl who was now staring at him shocked and terrified. Her green eyes wide open, her heart beating like crazy. He saw blood pouring down her neck and he offered help but she started running away. For a moment he wanted to let her go but then he saw her falling. He grabbed her right before she hit the pavement. She was unconscious so he took the girl inside and put her on the couch in the living room. Her wounds were already all healed, after all, it was a magical wound. He sat next to her for a minute just looking at her but she was not waking up so he took off her scarf, hat and boots and covered her legs with a blanket. He knew she was going to wake up with a headache as she lost lots of blood, so he brought a bottle of water from the kitchen and put it on the coffee table by the couch. He found some painkillers which he didn't even know he had and put them on the table next to the bottle of water, even though they passed their due date a few years before. He cleaned her neck with a wet towel to get rid of the rest of the blood, then he grabbed a glass of bourbon and a book and sat in the armchair by the couch, without paying any more attention to the girl. He knew what was going to happen next: she would wake up all confused and scared and he would calm her down, assuring her that whatever she thought she saw was untrue. Then, he would call her a taxi and they would never see each other again. She was just a human and Liam's all human acquaintances always ended in two ways: people either disappeared from his life running away in fear and horror or he left them without an explanation or a goodbye. There was never a third option.

An hour later Hayley came to. She sat on the couch and grabbed her head with both hands.

- Take the pills and drink some water. - Liam said - You are dehydrated, it will help.

Without hesitation, she took two pills and drank half a bottle of water. She was disoriented and shocked, looking at Liam and around the room, trying to remember how she got there in the first place.

- Don't worry, you're safe here. How are you feeling? - He sounded genuinely concerned.

- Dizzy... my head hurts.

- Do you remember what happened?

- I went out for a walk...

She touched her neck and looked at her hand as if she expected to see something there.

- No, I... I don't remember what happened.

Liam knew she was lying. At first, he wanted to stop at that and just let her go but then he thought about playing it a different way. Her fear and disbelieve would be more entertaining than any movie, besides, he had nothing to lose and he was bored.

- I think you do.

- No, that's impossible...

- What? That you were bitten by a vampire?

She looked at him terrified, stopped breathing and didn't even blink.

- What did you say?

But Liam didn't respond. Hayley didn't say anything for a couple of minutes, thinking about what Liam has just told her. Normally, she wouldn't believe in anything so ridiculous, but after that body turned into ashes, right there, right in front of her, she was eager to believe in any crazy theory.

- How can you know that? Are you a vampire hunter or something?

Liam hesitated with his answer. He didn't care about that girl and he didn't care what she thought. But for once, he wanted to be completely honest with somebody, no lies, no secrets. He wanted to say exactly what he wanted, without lying, without pretending to be someone else.

- Actually... I'm a vampire myself.

Hayley didn't say anything, she didn't even look at him. She was just staring at the empty bottle she was holding in her hands. '*He's going to kill me*' – she thought and her heart started beating significantly faster. Even though she was scared and felt completely hopeless, she didn't cry. She gazed at the door – '*There's no way I could reach that door in time, I'm too weak. I could scream but if he's really a vampire who's going to save me? Another vampire? What should I do? What's should I do?*'

- The door is open – he said - you are free to go whenever you want to.

'*Am I really or is he just playing with me? If it's a game maybe I should play along, buy myself some time.*'

Liam was sure she was about to start screaming or running - typical human reaction in a situation like that.

But Hayley was just sitting still, without a word, paralysed, deep in thought. A minute later, she finally spoke quietly, still staring at the bottle, not daring to look at Liam.

- Thank you for saving my life.

He couldn't believe it. He just told her he was a vampire and she was still sitting in front of him. No running, no screaming. *'Who is she? Is she a witch?'* he started to wonder.

- You're welcome... What's your name?

- Hayley. – she looked at Liam for a split second before she started staring at the bottle again.

- I'm Liam... Can I get you anything? More water?

Hayley didn't reply and just wrapped herself in a blanket.

- You're cold. Would you like some tea?

She nodded.

- I'll be right back.

Liam went to the kitchen and poured water into the kettle. He had so many questions and couldn't wait to find out more about Hayley. There was no human in the whole world that has shocked him like she did and all of a sudden, that evening became very interesting.

'This is my chance, I can run to the door now' – thought Hayley, but moving her head rapidly to have a quick look towards the kitchen was a mistake. The world around her spun and she lost her consciousness again. Liam brewed quickly some tea and came back to the living room but Hayley was lying on the couch already asleep and he decided not to wake her up. *'Who is she? Why didn't she run away?'* He was very confused. He stood there, looking at Hayley sleeping peacefully on his couch. She was pretty, probably in her early thirties, brown hair, slim and tall, a bit pale but it's probably because of what has happened earlier that evening.

- I wish we had met under different circumstances... Maybe you would have liked me.

Liam gently brushed her cheek with his fingers and went to his bedroom. He didn't fall asleep that night, instead, he was lying in his bed, listening to Hayley breathing, trying to figure out who she was. He was very curious and wanted to find out about her as much as he could. He just hoped that Isabella had nothing to do with it and their extraordinary meeting was just a pure coincidence.

When Liam got up in the morning, Hayley was still asleep. He stopped by the couch and looked at her and her peaceful face made him smile. He didn't want to wake her up so he decided to prepare some breakfast. *'Maybe she doesn't remember what I told her? Maybe she'll stay to eat so we could talk? Maybe she's different from the others?'* He went to the kitchen and started getting everything out of the fridge, preparing far too much food for just two of them. But he wanted to surprise her and make sure that there was at least one thing on that table that she liked. He couldn't remember the last time he had guests. Real guests, not just Isabella.

When Hayley woke up it was already bright outside, she must have slept through the whole night. She was glad the headache was gone and she felt much better. She sat on the couch and looked around the room: no photographs on the walls, no decorations, no plants, but the bookshelves were literally bending under the number of books and that caught Hayley's eye. *'How can someone have so many books?'* Although the walls were bright and warm and there were curtains in the windows and a carpet on the floor, the house didn't feel cosy. It was clearly missing a woman's touch and it didn't feel like home but more like a hotel. She heard Liam preparing breakfast in the kitchen. She got up slowly, still a bit dizzy and decided to play along, hoping he's going to let her go if she's nice to him. Her heart started beating faster and faster as her fear grew. When she appeared in the doorway, Liam looked at her with a smile. He looked like a regular nice guy and Hayley saw nothing unusual or extraordinary in his appearance.

- Good morning Hayley, how are you feeling?
- Much better, thank you.
- Would you like some breakfast?

He was perfectly polite, smiling, looking ordinary and normal so Hayley felt a bit more confident.

- If you don't mind, I'd like to go home now. I need to freshen up and...
- You don't have to explain yourself, you can go if want.

Liam put the empty plates down and walked Hayley to the front door. He was very disappointed even though he expected she could react that way. She obviously remembered everything that happened last night. He got his hopes too high again and maybe if he hadn't told her the truth she would have stayed. It was a stupid decision, he should have lied to her like he had to everybody else in the past.

- Would you like me to drive you home?
- No, thank you. I live nearby...Thank you again.

Hayley opened the door and walked out without hesitation. She caught a deep breath and started walking fast, not looking back. She turned around the corner and stopped, leaning against the wall. Nobody was following her and she was free to go home. There were people around her on the street and everything looked normal. *'Maybe he was not a psychopath? Maybe he really just wanted to save my life and his intentions were good?'* He put so much effort into preparing that breakfast for her and looked so disappointed when she left. And she was hungry, very much. She turned around and started slowly walking back feeling scared but also excited and curious. *'Whatever is meant to be, will be. If I'm to die today, I will die one way or another.'* Hayley believed in fate and destiny and although her common sense was telling her to run, her heart was telling her to go back, after all he saved her life and was helpful and polite, clearly meaning no harm. She hesitated just for a second before she opened the door without knocking. She looked at Liam sitting in the living room.

- I realised how rude it was of me to just walk away like that after you made that breakfast for me. Besides, I am really hungry.

Liam couldn't believe what was happening. *'Maybe she doesn't remember our conversation from last night after all? She just panicked as she was alone with a stranger. She just wanted to get out of that house, to get among other people on the street, to feel safe and make sure she was not held captive'.*

He got up from the couch and smiled.

- I didn't know what you liked so I made a bit of everything.

Hayley slowly followed him into the kitchen. There were eggs and beckon and toasts and jam and milk... Whatever could be served for breakfast, was on that table and it all looked and smelled very tasty. They sat down, facing each other and started eating.

- I hope there is at least one thing on this table that you like.

- Absolutely. Thank you, it all looks very delicious.

Hayley was watching Liam as he was putting food on his plate. She couldn't stop herself, she was too curious and she really wanted to get to know him.

- So you eat normal food too?

For a moment she regretted asking that question. First she acted then she thought and no matter how much she wanted to change, she couldn't, it was stronger than her. She kept making the same mistakes over and over again and she hated it. She looked at Liam, he seemed surprised. *'So she remembers, she knows... So why did she come back? Why is she so calm? Who is she?'*

- Yes, I eat and drink normally. I live my life like you do... I just need a bit of blood every now and then, that's all.

That went well. She was not terrified, he was not appalled by her question so it was safe to continue that topic.

- What else can you tell me?

- What would you like to know?

Liam didn't know what to tell Hayley as he didn't want to scare her away. They were both tense but tried to keep calm and create the impression that everything was ok. Hayley started pouring tea and continued their 'casual' conversation.

- Do you know Dracula and other similar books and movies? Can you tell me what is true and what is fiction?

- Well, let's see... Crosses, stakes and garlic - all fiction. I can also walk in the sun... I am very fast and strong and my senses are heightened... I also heal nearly instantly.

- So you're immortal then?

- Not exactly. A stronger vampire can kill a weaker one. Also, fire kills vampires... and magic... I would probably die if you chopped my head off... Never really seen anything like that myself, so I can't say for sure. - He smiled.

- Interesting...

Liam was so impressed. She looked fascinated, not scared and his answers amazed her, not terrified. Hayley was surprised how comfortable she started to feel in Liam's company. *'Maybe it's magic? Maybe all people feel that way?'*

- So... what are the cons? Is there anything you don't like about being... you?

He hesitated. All those things that he hated: being different, rejected by society, unloved, misunderstood and lonely, especially lonely. But she seemed so fascinated and he didn't want to take that away from her.

- What is there not to like? I am an improved version of a human being, powerful and invincible.

She liked that answer, it was easy to tell.

- So... how old are you if I may ask?

- I stopped counting long time ago, but if you wish to calculate yourself, I can tell you that I was born in seventeen fifty-five.

- Wow! All that history you must have seen. That's fascinating. You should write a book.

- Yes, I admit it's pretty amazing how much the world has changed throughout time. It's hard to get used to sometimes. Some years were better than the others.

- Is there any particular year you miss? Any time in the history that you would like to go back to?

He didn't expect that question and really didn't know what to say. Never thought about it before. Hayley looked at her watch and panicked.

- Oh gosh! It's already ten! I need to go, I need to feed my dog. Thank you very much for the breakfast, it was delicious.

- You're welcome.

Hayley took one last sip of her tea and got up.

- Thank you, Liam. I am really grateful for saving my life. If there is anything I can do to at least partially pay you back...

- Have a dinner with me. You can pay me back with your time, your company. I really wish to get to know you better.

- Oh...OK... - Hayley looked surprised - I think I can do that. I can never remember my own number though so why won't you give me yours and I will text you later so we can discuss that dinner idea?

Liam handed over his card. He really wanted to believe Hayley but deep down in his heart he knew he would never see her again.

- Till we meet again then? - He said.

- Sure. Bye.

Hayley was walking home fast. Excited and fascinated. *'I've just had a breakfast with a vampire, how weird is* that?' She couldn't wait to get back home. Poor dog, all by herself since yesterday evening, she was probably hungry and scared. When Hayley got home, Lexi was out of control, barking and jumping all around, so happy to see Hayley again.

- I am so sorry my dear but you would never believe what has happened to me.

Hayley gave Lexi some food, let her out into the garden and went to take a bath. When she was telling Lexi what has happened to her, she realised how incredibly it sounded. It was ridiculous! She could tell her dog about it but nobody else. Nobody would believe her anyway, she couldn't believe it herself. April and June would think she was losing her mind, they wouldn't believe her for sure. Liam's secret was safe with Hayley then. She had nobody to tell. Even with the two small scars clearly visible on her neck, she wouldn't be able to convince anyone that vampires existed.

Hayley couldn't bother to cook so she went for a takeaway. She took Lexi for a long well-deserved walk, played with her and got carried away. It was already evening when she finally got time to relax on her couch with Lexi lying by her side.

- Should I text him Lexi? I promised I would... But obviously, he would understand if I didn't... He saved my life, I thanked him and that's the end of the story. There is nothing I can do to pay him back, really. After all, he saved my life... But we live so close... what if we met on the street or at the store? What would I tell him then? That I lost his number? That I forgot where he lived? Lame excuse, he would know it would be a lie. But he's so... interesting and fascinating... and there is so much he could tell me... seventeen fifty-five… that's so much history to tell… All these things he must have seen.

She held Liam's card in one hand and her cell phone in the other. She looked at her dog as if she actually expected Lexi to tell her what to do. Hayley had a good feeling about Liam. He saved her life, took good care of her and she really wanted to see him again. She didn't think of him as a monster. How could he be a mystical beast and be so nice and caring at the same time? If he hadn't told her the truth, she would never think he could be a bad guy. He didn't do anything wrong and Hayley didn't want to punish him just for being honest with her. He didn't have to help her but he did and all he wanted in return was a chat over dinner. She could do that much, it didn't cost her anything and she felt obliged to thank him for saving her life. She took a deep breath, unlocked her phone and typed Liam's number.

Liam spent the whole day thinking about Hayley and waiting for her call. She was his dream come true, everything he ever wanted. She accepted him for what he was, talked to him with no fear or disgust. And she was beautiful, those green eyes were so charming, full of life and light. Through all his long life, there was no human like Hayley. With her, for the first time in years, he felt good about himself and didn't feel the need to change anything, to become someone else. Even if she was not interested in being with him, she could still be a friend, a great person to have around.

He was sitting in his chair with a drink but no book as he couldn't focus on reading, being deep in thought about Hayley. Isabella came unexpectedly, opening the door as if it was her own house. He didn't even hear her parking her car outside.

- Hi brother. Are you OK?

- As a matter of fact, I am.

Isabella froze for a minute, looking at Liam with her jaw down. She couldn't believe it, her brother was smiling. He was sitting right there, looking at her with a genuine smile on his face.

- O my god. You're smiling! For the first time in years, you seem happy.

- Because I am happy.

- Tell me, what's happened?

- I met someone, a very unique girl. Her name is Hayley and she is truly extraordinary.

Isabella sat down, ready for a good story.

- Who is she? Where did you meet her? Tell me everything!

- I met her yesterday evening. She was attacked outside my window and I saved her life.

- So... she's human?

- Yes, but she's unlike anyone else.

Isabella rolled her eyes.

- Oh Liam, don't do this again. It always ends the same way. The moment they find out...

- She knows.

- What?!

- She already knows.

- I don't understand. How come she knows?

- Because I told her.

- Hold on. So you met a girl and told her you were a vampire?

- Well, there is more to it but yes, pretty much. Some vampire bit her so I killed him and saved her life. She passed out so I brought her here and when she came to, we talked. In the morning, we had some breakfast, we talked a bit more and she went home. We will meet again soon, I gave her my number and she will call me later so we can make proper arrangements.

Isabella didn't believe a single word Liam has just said. He must have smoked something or drunk something or was under a spell. Whatever it was, that girl was not real.

- My dear brother, this is impossible. Do you hear yourself? This has never happened, that girl is not real.

- You're wrong. You'll meet her, once we have that dinner arranged, I will let you know and you'll meet her so you can see for yourself.

- OK… Let's say it's all real and it all happened. Do you really think she will call you? Do you really believe she would like to see you again? Now, that she's back home she probably just wants to forget all about it.

Liam didn't say anything, Isabella was right and their extraordinary story was over. Hayley was never going to give him her number, it would be too good to be true. He was about to admit that out loud to Isabella, but then his cell phone made a sound, he received a text message.

- Was it a good decision? It was, wasn't it?

Hayley waited for Lexi to talk to her but the dog just looked at her puzzled. After long thinking, Hayley has sent that message, it was short:

'Hi Liam. This is my number. I will let you know when I'm free for that dinner. Will call you tomorrow. Thanks again. Hayley'

It felt right. She needed someone new in her life, she couldn't spend every free moment with her dog, that would eventually drive her crazy. And who was a better companion than her saviour? Yes, he was a vampire but she didn't really know what it truly meant. She couldn't just assume he was a blood-thirsty monster, after all, he saved her life and let her go. She couldn't believe that someone so charming, handsome and nice was just simply evil. She felt it was unfair to base her knowledge on books and movies that were a pure fiction and nothing more. How could she do that, not giving Liam a chance to properly explain to her what being a vampire really meant. She was not looking for a relationship and she was not picturing herself as Liam's girlfriend. All she wanted was a friend, someone to talk to, someone to go for a walk with. She has realised how much she talked to Lexi and it started to scare her and annoy her. She needed another human being in her life, even if that someone was not human at all.

Hayley heard the doorbell the moment she was letting Lexi out into the garden. It was a woman, probably in her twenties, tall, slim, blond with blue eyes. Hayley has never seen her before and yet, she looked familiar.

- Can I help you?

The woman was staring at Hayley without a word. Then, she looked at her neck.

- So it's true...you must be Hayley.

- And you are?

- I'm Isabella, Liam's sister.

'*Liam never mentioned he had a sister. Is she really his sister? Why is she here? How did she find me?*' There were some many questions running through Hayley's head at that moment but she picked only one.

- How did you know where I lived?

- I have my ways of finding people. I need to talk to you about what happened, is that OK?

Hayley thought for a moment and then asked Isabella to come in. The girl immediately cut to the chase.

- I heard an unbelievable story about how my brother met you and about your time together and I just wanted to verify if it's true.

'What does she want to verify? Why would Liam lie to her? Why is she really here?'

- OK... What do you want to know?

They sat at the table in the kitchen. Hayley didn't offer Isabella anything to drink, she was afraid and tense and Isabella sensed that.

- So, what happened? I see you have some marks on your neck. Are they from yesterday?

- Yes, I was attacked.

- Do you remember who attacked you?

- I don't remember his face, never seen him before. As it turned out, it was a vampire, but I assume this is not the unbelievable part you wanted to verify.

- No, it's not. – Isabella was surprised that Hayley still wanted to talk to her despite clearly being scared - So what happened next?

- I passed out and when I came to, I was in Liam's house. He took care of me.

- Did he tell you anything... unexpected? Shocking?

- He said he's a vampire and if you really are his sister then I assume you are one too.

They looked at each other without a word and Hayley started feeling overwhelmed by the growing fear. It was stupid of her to let Isabella in. Lexi was in the backyard, she didn't even bark. Obviously, she wouldn't be able to protect Hayley but she would at least make her feel less frightened. Isabella was genuinely surprised. She didn't expect Hayley to be so straightforward and most of all, she didn't expect Liam's story to be true, but it obviously was. The girl he talked about was real.

- And then you stayed for the night and had some breakfast the next day?

- Yes.

- You see, that's the part I don't understand. You were attacked by a vampire, nearly killed, then, you found out the guy who saved you was also a vampire. You were in his house so why didn't it scare you?

- What was I supposed to do?

- I don't know. Run, scream, cry?

- I lost lots of blood, I had a terrible headache, I was dizzy and weak and I could barely sit straight. How was I supposed to run? And even if I had screamed, who would have saved me anyway? There was no way I could have picked up a fight with a regular guy so what was I supposed to do with a real vampire?

Isabella didn't say anything so Hayley continued.

- Normally, I would have assumed he was joking or just trying to scare me... But after that attack... I remembered how that man got his heart torn out and how he turned into ashes right there in front of my eyes. I knew what I saw. It was unbelievable, but it was real.

- So you were scared?

- Of course I was scared. I was terrified! I was sure I was about to die that night. But I felt so powerless and I thought there was nothing I could have done. But thankfully, it all turned out well. Liam was perfectly nice to me and took good care of me. When I came to in the morning and I was still alive and the door was unlocked, I realised he's intentions were good. I felt a bit more confident seeing other people outside on the street so I stayed for breakfast.

Isabella was still struggling to understand.

- But you were attacked! How could you trust Liam knowing he's exactly the same monster that nearly killed you earlier that night?

- The man who attacked me was a real monster, he wanted to kill me, he hurt me really bad. But Liam is not a monster, he was kind to me. They are not the same.

- But they're both vampires.

- Let me put it this way: if you were bitten by a Pitbull, would you be afraid of a Labrador too? Our would you know that there are some aggressive and dangerous dogs you should avoid and some friendly dogs that you could trust and play with?

Isabella looked at Hayley with a gentle smile.

- Liam was right about you. You really are extraordinary.

- What do you mean?

Hayley was less scared now seeing that smile, it looked genuine. It was clear that Isabella didn't come over looking for a fight, she just wanted to see if Liam had told her the truth. But Hayley couldn't understand why Isabella didn't trust her own brother and why it was so important to verify his story.

- Let me give you a bit of a background, so you can understand better and I hope Liam won't be angry with me for telling you all this. You see, Liam doesn't like being a vampire. I got the impression that he hated it from the very beginning. With time, he got used to it but never truly accepted it. He believed, however, that if people could accept him, he could accept himself too. But nobody would...

Isabella thought for a moment before she decided to continue. She looked at Hayley who was listening to her carefully. She didn't seem afraid anymore but curious.

- He was in love a few times. Once, he even got married but right after the ceremony he told his wife the truth. He thought she really loved him and that she would accept him for what he was. After all, she promised to be with him forever, no matter what. But she called him a monster, packed her bags and ran away the same day. He never saw her again. Second time, he told his girlfriend the truth right after engagement. He didn't want to go on with the wedding that time, without making sure it was real love. Same situation. She called him names and disappeared. Years later, he met another girl. He really loved her and cared for her so he didn't want to say anything. But the girl had a feeling he was hiding something from her. She was ensuring him she would love him no matter what and she wanted him to be completely honest with her. So he told her. She called him names, even a devil himself, and that truly broke Liam's heart. And so he realised there was no love for him, that he could never be with anyone so he got very miserable. I haven't seen him smiling in years and today he smiled. He told me about you and I didn't believe him. Now, you can understand why. But you are real and the story is true and I find it hard to believe even though you are right in front of me.

Hayley took a moment to process those stories Isabella has just told her. She didn't expect to find out so much at once. She decided to use this short moment of honesty and ask Isabella a very important question. The one that she had in her head from the moment she sent that text message to Liam.

- I have a question... You see, I am supposed to have this dinner with him. I thought I could go out with him that one time as a 'thank you for saving my life' and that would be it. I know I said he was nice to me but...I just can't stop wondering... Does he kill people?

Isabella was surprised to hear that. She didn't expect Hayley would actually ask her that question.

- No, we are not murderers. We have a friend working in a hospital, he supplies us with the blood bags.

Hayley really wanted to believe Isabella and she sounded very convincing but how could she trust her?

- OK, good to hear that... But that's how it is now... and what was it like in the past?

Hayley wanted to find out as much as she could and she thought it was her only chance to get some answers.

She was watching Isabella carefully, looking for any signs of a lie.

- Liam killed one person shortly after he was turned. We both did, actually. We didn't know what we were and the hunger was overwhelming so we attacked a man and killed him. When we realised what's happened we thought we were possessed or cursed so we turned to our friend Leah who was a witch. She saw how terrified and full of remorse we were and understood there was still hope for us. She didn't think of us as monsters and she used her magic to help us control the hunger. It helped us hunt without killing anyone and she made sure we would never lose control ever again. So I can assure you Liam would never hurt you unintentionally. Or intentionally, as a matter of fact. I can assure you he's a good guy.

- I saw him killing another vampire.

- That's different. Besides, he didn't kill one of the good guys, it was either you or that guy and Liam made his choice. Luckily for you.

Hayley sat there quietly, thinking. How could she believe Isabella? She didn't know her. Isabella just didn't want to see her brother heartbroken again so she would say whatever Hayley wanted to hear. But Hayley wanted to believe her, she liked Liam, there was something fascinating about him and she really wanted to believe that he was good.

- Thanks for telling me all this.

- No problem. I thought being honest with you would help you make right decisions. He really likes you, you know? Even though you have just met and exchanged only a few words, it's easy to say that you got his interest and he got yours. Don't judge him too hastily.

Isabella looked at her watch.

- I'll be going now. Nice talking to you Hayley and I hope to see you again. Probably at that dinner you will have with Liam, I'm sure he will invite me over to prove me you're real. Goodnight Hayley.

Hayley made sure she locked the door after Isabella left. It was stupid of her to let a stranger in and she promised herself she would never do that again. She went to the garden and let Lexi inside. The dog started walking around the kitchen, sniffing. She knew someone was there and she was running around the house trying to find the source of that new, unknown smell.

- She's not here anymore, you silly dog. Come here.

They sat on the couch and Hayley turned the TV on and tried to relax but she was deep in thought.

- Another vampire… how many more am I about to meet? How many are there? If vampires are real, are other magical creatures real too? What about werewolves or elves? Isabella said their friend was a witch… Unbelievable… I can't believe magic is real. I've spent thirty years not experiencing anything magical and now I'm being told impossible is in fact possible… Is there anything truly impossible anymore?

Liam was so happy to see Hayley's text. But what if she was under a spell? What if Isabella had found a witch and planned it all? Was any of it real? His sister was ready to do anything to help him but would she go that far? He realised that he was on the right track to lose his mind so he decided not to think too much about it anymore and just try to enjoy Hayley's company. There was something interesting about her, in the way she reacted that night and the next morning.

They planned dinner for Saturday. As they wanted to speak freely, they decided to meet at Liam's. How could they talk about vampires in the restaurant among strangers? How could they truly be themselves in a public space like that? Liam wanted to be himself and was ready to talk about everything, not afraid of what questions Hayley might ask. He promised himself he would give her only honest answers and he would not hold anything back. He had a chance to be perfectly honest with someone from the very beginning and he didn't want to ruin it. He knew he already lied once telling Hayley there was nothing he didn't like about being a vampire but it was a harmless lie and he was ready to let that one go.

It was Saturday evening and Liam waited impatiently for his guests to arrive. He ordered Thai food and wine and Hayley was supposed to bring some dessert. He put on his smart shirt and jeans trying not to look too formal. He sprayed himself with perfumes and combed his hair. For the first time in many years, he felt anxious, as if he was about to have a job interview. He wanted to impress Hayley and was afraid that he may say something that would drive her away. He was looking at his reflection in the mirror, taking deep breaths.

- You're an idiot – he said to himself staring back at his reflection. - Just relax and have some fun. She's a lovely girl and she's going to like you. You can't mess it up, she already knows the worst part.

Liam heard the door opening downstairs. It was Isabella, she showed up a little bit earlier as she wanted to talk to Liam alone.

- I'm glad you came after all, I wasn't sure you would, considering you think I made that girl up. – said Liam going down the stairs.

- There is something I need to tell you brother... I already met Hayley. I went to see her in her house that day.

Liam didn't say anything. He looked angry.

- I just wanted to verify your story. Don't worry I didn't tell her anything to scare her away. Actually, I think it's good I had that chat with her. She had a few questions about you and I think I helped her make the right decision. You were right brother, she really is unique.

Before Liam commented on that, Hayley knocked on the door. He was glad to see her again. She looked beautiful in her black dress, very elegant and completely different to how he remembered her. She wasn't pale anymore, her hair wasn't in a mess and her clothes were not covered in blood.

- Good evening Hayley, come in. I believe you already had a pleasure to meet my dear sister Isabella.

They looked at each other with a gentle smile and sat at the table. Liam poured the wine and brought the food. They were all a bit tense at the beginning but within a half an hour, they felt more comfortable and found it easy to talk to each other, after all. They ate, joked and talked about work, friends, dogs, the movies they watched and books they read. Everything seemed normal. Nobody said a single word about vampires or witches and the evening was fun. The most fascinating topic was Isabella's job as she was a bounty hunter. It was a good job for a vampire as she could use her special abilities to track her bounties down. Liam turned out to be a writer and history was his speciality as he was good in remembering the past with vivid details. He has published his books under different names, throughout time. He couldn't be John Smith for hundreds of years so he was changing his alias every few decades. Different names, different cities and even countries. Their life seemed so fascinating to Hayley who was just a psychologist, a widow with a dog. She didn't have many interesting stories but she enjoyed listening and those two had a lot to say. It seemed like they have been everywhere, seen everything and experienced everything. All those crazy things they've done – it all sounded so exciting and Hayley envied them the amazing lives they led.

- I think it's time for me to go now, it' getting late – Hayley got up realising it was nearly eleven o'clock - I had a really great time today.

- Would you like me to walk you home? - Liam asked.

It was dark outside so Hayley was glad Liam offered to walk her home. With him by her side, nobody would dare to accost her.

- If you don't mind, I don't live far but I would love some company.

The evening was cold but it was not snowing and the starry sky over their heads made their walk even more pleasant.

- So… - Liam started - I wanted to get to know you a bit better and instead you just found out more about me and Isabella. Don't get me wrong, I had a great time, but it was not exactly what I expected. After these few hours I honestly still don't know anything about you. So who's Hayley Evans?

- OK, let me summarize my life for you then. It's much shorter than yours so there is not much to say. I am thirty-four years old, a psychologist with two younger twin sisters April and June and a dog called Lexi. I like playing guitar, skiing and horse riding. I am also a great cook and I love baking... How about that?

Liam smiled.

- Great, I already feel like I know you a little better. You painted here a really good picture of yourself, Hayley even though you come across as a little shy. I may not know much about you but what I do already know makes you sound very interesting. So tell me, would you like to have another dinner with me? Without Isabella this time, just the two of us so we can have a proper conversation.

Hayley thought for a moment. One dinner with Liam and his sister was just a nice way to introduce themselves to each other but what Liam has proposed now sounded like a real date. She was not ready for another relationship, especially with an immortal magical creature but she liked Liam and wanted to spend some more time with him, hoping they could be friends one day.

- How about my place then? I hate leaving Lexi alone and I could cook something.

- Sounds perfect.

Liam waited for her to get inside, before he turned around and started walking away. '*What a gentleman*' – Hayley thought, looking at Liam as she was locking the door. She went to the kitchen and started going through her recipe book, thinking what to cook for their next dinner together. Meeting Liam was the most fascinating thing that happened to her in a very long time and it consumed all her attention. She couldn't wait to see him again, to hear more of his amazing stories. His life was so full of excitement and adventure and she envied him that. She envied that he could live his life to the fullest not worrying about the future, knowing he would never run out of time. Being a vampire sounded like a great way to go through life and Hayley couldn't wait to find out what it was truly like for him.

Chapter 4

Liam was now preparing to leave for his next dinner with Hayley. That one week has passed very slowly for him as he waited impatiently for another Saturday. He put on jeans and a black shirt, leaving the first two buttons undone.

- I want to give Leah's ring to Hayley. - Liam said to Isabella as she was watching him getting ready.

- OK, do it. In case she runs away without a goodbye, I will hunt her down and take the ring back.

Isabella was obviously joking, she liked Hayley and had a good feeling about her.

- She won't run away, I think we're getting on quite well, actually. Not sure how she feels about me exactly but I can tell she likes me.

Isabella has seen that look full of optimism before. Every time Liam got his hopes too high, he ended up heartbroken, disappointed and angry. She didn't want to see him like that again and although she wanted him to enjoy his time with Hayley, she needed him to remember it was just for now and there was no future these two could share. But Liam knew that already and a thought of losing Hayley was constantly in his head. He knew she was not promised tomorrow and her time would end and one way or another, she would die. If not an accident or illness, time would eventually take her away. But he didn't want to ruin his evening with Hayley by thinking about the future. Now was good and he wanted to focus on that. They have just met and it was far too early to think about what's yet to come. But he always did that. He always ruined his present by thinking about the future or reminiscing about the past. No more. He decided he would enjoy every minute together with Hayley and he would let himself be truly happy for once.

Hayley's house was very homely, specious, bright and colourful. There were many photos on the wall and some green plants in the corners. Although the walls were pastel-coloured, there were many accessories in bright colours everywhere around the house. Starting from colourful cushions on the comfy sofa and fluffy rug on the floor in the living room, ending on the various green kitchen accessories like apron, gloves and tea towels. It was one of those places people wanted to go back to after a hard day at work, a true home full of happy memories, cozy, warm and safe. It was an exact opposite of Liam's house which felt cold and empty and even though it was stylish and expensive, it felt more like a prison than a home.

- I like your house, Hayley. It looks much better than mine. - said Liam having a quick look around the living room.

- Thank you, I know it's very girly but I like these bright colours.

- I think it looks very cosy. I see you visited many places. It looks like your whole life is on these walls.

- I like looking at these photographs, they remind me of people I used to know and great time I had on all these trips. I am very sentimental.

- So am I.

Hayley led Liam to the kitchen.

- I didn't know what you like and I didn't want to bring to this table anything you wouldn't enjoy so I decided to make a pizza. I know it sounds simple and easy but I always put a lot of heart into preparing dinners for others so I hope at the end of this evening, you will honestly admit it was one of the best pizzas you have ever had.

- I'm sure you're right. It's smells very delicious.

Hayley prepared an excellent dinner and it was flawless. The whole evening was perfect. They ate and laughed and there was not a single second of silence. They were perfect together, talking like old friends.

- Hayley, I have something for you.

Liam reached out to his pocket and handed Leah's ring to Hayley.

- Don't worry, it's not a proposal, it's a gift. My dear friend Leah gave it to me and it is magical. She put a spell on it so whoever wears it seems to be a vampire to other vampires. They won't be attracted to you and you'll be safer. I want you to have it.

Hayley looked at the ring, it was beautiful. Silver band with little diamonds around an emerald stone.

- Thank you Liam, it's beautiful... But unfortunately it's far too large for my skinny fingers.

Liam took Hayley's hand and put the ring on her finger. It instantly got smaller to fit Hayley's finger perfectly.

- Like I said, it's magical.

It was the first time Hayley felt Liam's touch and her heart skipped a beat.

- Forgive me, I should not have done this. - said Liam seeing the look on Hayley's face.

- Don't be silly, you just surprised me, that's all. Besides, I have never worn a magical ring before.

But Liam felt that electricity too and he knew it had nothing to do with the ring. He started worrying that even though Hayley seemed to enjoy his company, she was still afraid of him.

- So, who's Leah? - Hayley found a way out of that awkward moment.

- She was like a sister to me and Isabella and we spent our childhood together. It was fun because Leah was a witch and she showed us all the spells and tricks her mother has taught her. It was never boring with Leah. She lived for nearly two hundred years using magic to slow down the ageing process and to keep herself healthy. But she got tired at some point and decided that she bought herself enough time to discover the world and there was nothing more left. Eternity was not for her. Besides, she wanted to see her family again, to reconnect with her ancestors and return her magic to the earth. I still miss her. She was the only one who truly accepted me and Isabella for who we were. She was very helpful and very supportive. Amazing friend. I wish you knew her, I think you two would like each other.

- I can't believe she gave up an eternal life and decided to die.

- It may seem weird to you because you've only lived a few decades, but for someone who's been around for more than a lifetime, it is a good decision.

- Have you ever thought about dying? - Hayley asked without hesitation. It was one of those moments when she acted before she thought – I'm sorry, I shouldn't have asked that and you don't have to answer.

Liam looked at Hayley not saying anything but thinking. He hesitated with his answer but he promised himself he would not build that relationship on a lie and he would be honest with Hayley so she could get to know him, the real him.

- Yes – he eventually responded – I thought about it once or twice because it doesn't matter how great your life may seem to the others, sometimes it's just not good enough for you. You may think my life is perfect because I am strong, fearless, rich and not limited by time or illness but even Hollywood stars commit suicide and you may think they have everything. Sometimes everything is not enough, especially when you have nobody to share it with. I've never had a real and honest relationship with anybody. When Leah died, I was left without any real friends. In my lowest moments, Isabella was the only one keeping me alive. I couldn't just leave her all alone, she wouldn't survive without me. Even though she doesn't spend much time with me and it seems like she doesn't need me, it brings her comfort knowing that I am somewhere out there and she could visit anytime she wants.

- I completely understand… As we are being honest with each other, I think I should let you know that I also wanted to die once. When my husband died, I didn't want to live all alone and it was very difficult for me to keep going. But I have two sisters I feel responsible for and I know they have only me and I can't leave them alone. So I fought my grief and depression and stayed strong for them. But I know what it means when your life shatters into pieces and you feel like there is no point in moving forward. I can understand why people feel this way even if their lives may seem perfect.

They spent the rest of the evening talking. Liam didn't want to leave and Hayley didn't want him to go. Before they even realised what time it was, they heard birds outside and it was already dawn.

Chapter 5

Weeks were passing by fast. Monday to Friday Hayley was swamped with her work but every weekend she spent with Liam. She liked her life that way, especially that Liam was very entertaining. They didn't go any fancy places but Hayley didn't need that, they could have fun at home just watching movies or talking. And there was always something to talk about.

One day, Hayley decided to surprise Liam. She wanted to take him to the mountains as the weather was perfect for hiking even though it was cold and there were still traces of snow in the shade. It was end of March and the spring was coming earlier that year. She packed her backpack, prepared stuff for Lexi and headed to Liam's. She didn't knock as Liam was always telling her she could come in whenever she wanted, the door was always open and even if he was not home, she could wait inside. When she opened the door she saw Liam and Isabella arguing. Liam looked at Hayley and immediately turned his face away. For the first time, for a split second, Hayley saw what he really looked like as a vampire. His usually blue eyes were completely black and contrasted even more with his pale face. There were thick dark veins under his eyes and he looked freighting. Without a word, Hayley turned around and started walking away.

- Hayley! Hayley! wait! - Isabella ran after her.

Hayley stopped. She looked scared.

- I should have knocked.

- Don't be silly, sooner or later you would see it. It had to happen at some point.

Hayley was frightened so Isabella grabbed her by the hand and pulled her aside, making sure that nobody was watching them.

- Look at me.

Hayley looked at Isabella's face and saw the same dark veins showing up. Then, her blue eyes turned black. Lexi hid behind Hayley with a quiet growl.

- You see? I look different but it's still me. It's me, Hayley. You don't have to be afraid.

Next second, her face came back to normal and she let go of Hayley's hand.

- You're right...I just forgot... We have known each other for months and that topic never came up. There was always something else to talk about and I have completely forgotten you're... Never mind. I'm fine, I promise.

- You're sure?

- Yes, all good.

- Are you OK to go back with me now?

- Yes. I wanted Liam to go hiking with me and Lexi. We still can do that... I think.

- Great, let's go back then.

They started walking slowly back to Liam's. Hayley was taking deep breaths. '*Why am I reacting this way? It's not like I didn't know so why did it shock me that much?*'

- Come on Liam, we are going hiking. Can we take your car?

He stood there for a minute trying to understand what she has just said.

- Yes! Of course. Give me two minutes.

Hayley went outside and closed the door behind her. She didn't want to talk about it but she knew they would have to at some point. It was a big deal. She never saw a monster in him but those eyes really frightened her and it was not something they could just easily leave under the carpet.

It was a short drive so they managed to talk about everything else and the journey was not that bad. They parked their car, took their backpacks and started to walk..

- Liam, I want to talk about that situation earlier. We have known each other for months and we spent a lot of time together. The whole point of me knowing... the truth... was so that you could feel comfortable around me and you didn't have to hide. I accepted the fact that you are... different... without actually having any proof of it being true. So I need to know what you really look like and I need to be OK with that. So... can you show me again so I can have a proper look? I am ready this time so I will not freak out again, I promise.

Liam was not sure about that being a good idea but he wanted to be accepted for what he was and he needed Hayley to feel comfortable around him. He looked at her and his face was serious. First, she saw the veins, then his eyes turned black. Just like Isabella's. They kept looking at each other for a few seconds without a word.

- Please, say something Hayley.

- Well.... Honestly? - Hayley was looking for the right words. - You look very scary...Great for Halloween, by the way.

Liam laughed. His face was human again.

- You always know the right words, don't you Hayley?

- So when do you turn? I mean, what makes you change?

- When I'm very scared or angry... or hungry. But as you can see I can change at will too.

- So what was it today?

- I was angry. Isabella brought me some bad news and it made me angry. Normally we would have heard you coming but we were so engaged in that conversation that we totally ignored all sounds in the background. But I will keep in mind that I have a human friend now so I need to control myself.

- And I will keep in mind that I have a vampire friend so ... I should always knock.

Liam laughed again. Everything was fine, back to normal.

They were hiking for a couple of hours now. Although Hayley was in a good shape, she couldn't keep up with Liam and Lexi always being a few steps ahead. She envied them being so full of energy.

- Do you ever get tired, Liam? – she asked breathing heavily and wiping the sweat from her forehead.

- Not really. I assume if I didn't sleep for a few days then maybe I'll be tired. But I never tested that theory.

- Lucky you. I don't think I will have any energy left to get back to the car. I think we'll sit here, get some food and rest and then we can start walking back.

They sat on the ground, leaning against a fallen tree. There was nobody around, even birds were unusually quiet that day. Many wild animals didn't leave their hideaways yet as it was still quite cold. The whole forest was waiting for the spring to come. Hayley had a look around to make sure nobody was listening.

- Liam… Isabella told me you've always hated your life. Why?

Liam was surprised with that question. He didn't know Hayley knew that and it was surprising that she didn't bring that up earlier. He started to wonder what else she knew and kept unsaid.

- Not always. There were episodes in my life when I loved it. I was reckless, I jumped from incredibly high cliffs straight into a deep, dark ocean, or I stood face to face with wild animals, looking them straight in the eye. I have done some fascinating things that I couldn't have done while being human. I was pushing the boundaries, checking my limits. It was fun.

- So what changed? Why were you so unhappy?

- I wanted a family, home, normal life. But we had to move around a lot so people didn't notice we were not getting older. Isabella is a free spirit, she doesn't look for home, she can be happy wherever she is. But I am not like her. And so I realised I would be forever alone and I hated that idea.

- Was that the only thing that made you hate your life? What about the hunger and the idea of drinking blood?

- The hunger was easily controlled thanks to Leah and it was not an issue. Once I've turned the blood seemed to be the most desirable food. I wanted it and the idea of drinking it only brought me joy.

- So speaking hypothetically, if there was a spell to reverse it all, would you like to be human again?

Liam hesitated with an answer.

- No.

Hayley furrowed her brow confused.

- But you said you hated it.

- It's complicated, not so much black and white as you think. There was a time in my life when I would have done anything to be human again. I was afraid of loneliness and the idea of an eternal life frightened me. But thinking about it now, I believe I would be more afraid of being weak and helpless. I got used to feeling invincible. I feel better knowing that I would never get old, never run out of time, never get sick...

The more Liam was talking the more Hayley got depressed. He made her realise how much it sucked to be human, to know that every day may be the last one, that the clock was ticking and with every minute she was closer to death. She hated it how quickly she got tired or how pathetic she felt every time she was ill.

- How can a human become a vampire?

- Their heart needs to stop while there is a vampire blood in their system. They die for a few minutes to come back to life as vampires... Hayley, you're not asking this because you would like to become one, right?

Hayley didn't answer. So it was possible, she could be like him if she wanted to. There was a way to change everything that she hated about herself.

- Hayley, I know I said a few cool things about it and it sounded interesting and exciting but it still means that your friends and family will die and you'll live forever.

- You and Isabella are my friends and you'll never die. I could stick with you and never feel lonely.

- Would that be enough though? What about a husband? A baby? Don't you want a family of your own?

He was right, she could never have that as a vampire. She loved her house and her job and she didn't want to move. She spent her whole life in that town. And how could she leave April and June? How would she explain that to them?

- You're right Liam, I was just curious, that's all. Don't worry, I don't plan on dying any time soon... Let's go home.

Nearly three hours later, they were back at Hayley's. She was half-alive and her feet hurt. The moment Lexi lay down on the floor, she immediately fell asleep. Liam was the same as he was that morning. Nothing changed. No sweat, no sign of being tired at all.

- I hate to be rude but I will ask you to leave now. I need to take a shower and go to bed, otherwise I will just hit the floor like my dog.

Liam smiled.

- Goodnight Hayley. I'll see you next week.

Chapter 6

It was fifteenth of April, exactly six months since Hayley met Liam and Isabella. It was a cold October evening when she was attacked. Now, everything was waking up after winter and Hayley loved spring. People got less depressed during that time, days were getting longer and warmer, the sky was less cloudy and the first flowers started showing up. Hayley was sitting in the park, enjoying the sunshine and watching Lexi running with a ball. She was thinking about her life, what it has been like for the last six months and how different it was from the last year. She was so sure she would never be happy again when her world shattered into pieces after her husband died. She felt miserable and her life had no meaning. Now, she had an amazing friend who turned her world upside down but in a good way. It was exactly what she needed - to be moved to the bone, terrified, made sure she was going to die and even though it was a horrifying evening when she was attacked, fate put on her path an amazing man, her saviour, her best friend. Now, she spent every free moment with him, a person who made her feel safe, appreciated and needed. She was in a good place in her life now and her sisters didn't have to worry about her anymore. April and June met Liam and Isabella at Christmas but they didn't know the truth about them of course. How could they? There was no right way to bring such news. Hayley practiced many times a different way of telling her sisters that her best friend was a vampire but every sentence she used sounded ridiculous or scary so she eventually gave up. But they didn't need to know, they were just glad to see their big sister happy again and her wellbeing was all that mattered. Every time Hayley was with Liam, it was as if they were both just normal people. Hiking, skiing, watching movies, having dinners - nothing unusual about that. It was so easy to forget how much magic was actually involved as Liam's uniqueness has never impacted Hayley in any way. She has been spending recently a bit more time with him. Not only weekends but also every evening. She has had less work so Liam could join her for her long evening walks with Lexi. Hayley liked Liam's company. She liked when he was close. Every now and then, when their hands touched, there was a pleasant spark leaving her heart beating fast. Life was so much more enjoyable with Liam being around. Who knew that someone straight from a horror book could bring so much joy into one's life.

- Masquerade!
Isabella stormed in unexpectedly, nearly making Liam jump.
- What are you talking about?
- The ball! Music, dancing, good food. We're going!
The masquerade was hosted every year and it was for vampires only - a good way to get to know the community. Isabella loved it but Liam has not attended for a few years in a row. He used to love dancing but going there without a plus one was not a pleasant experience so he decided not to go at all.
- I don't think it's a good idea.
- Oh come on! You can take Hayley. She'd love it!
- Are you insane? How can I bring her there?
- She'll be wearing Leah's ring so nobody has to know she's human. Moreover, I think it's a good idea to introduce her to the community. She'd be safer if all vampires around knew she was our friend. I will talk to her, trust me, you two will have a great time.

Liam wasn't too sure about it. He wanted to keep Hayley hidden from the whole world, but Isabella was right, introducing Hayley to others could be beneficial. But before he decided to agree, Isabella stormed out and drove straight to Hayley's. She was very excited thinking about the ball. She loved good music and dancing and it would be nice to have Hayley and Liam around. She got out of the car and went inside without knocking as the door was unlocked.

- Hayley, do you like dancing?

Hayley jumped, slightly burning her hands and nearly dropping her bowl of soup. Lexi barked once before she realised who came in and then, she waved her tail and gave Isabella a proper welcome.

- Sure... I am not quite sure though if I am good at it. I dance only when I'm drunk and I bet it does not look good.

- You'll come dancing with me and Liam. There is this ball hosted in two weeks' time and I'm sure you'll love it! It's a masquerade, everyone will be dressed up. I attend every year. It's very posh and very unique.

- Is it here in Aspen? How come I've never heard of it?

- Well, it's for vampires only so it's a closed party and only those invited know about it. We got our invitations and you'll be Liam's plus one so they will let you in. You just need to be sure you'll be wearing that magical ring of yours so nobody knows you're human and it will be all just fine. You're perfectly safe with us, trust me. It's for your benefit and safety to introduce you to everyone.

- And what did Liam say?

- He thinks you wouldn't like to go.

- Let's prove him wrong then, shall we?

- That's the spirit! I knew you'd go.

- Tell me, what should I wear? I want to fit in.

- Don't worry, I will order you something nice. The ball starts at seven so we'll have plenty of time on the day to get ready. I will take care of you and you will look gorgeous! Leave it all with me.

- OK then. I put my trust in you, Isabella so don't let me make a fool of myself.

A ball full of vampires and nobody would know she was human. That sounded interesting and exciting but also a bit scary. *'A masquerade... Like in Phantom of the Opera... Or Great Gatsby. It sounds so magical'* And so the countdown started and Hayley couldn't wait. She couldn't remember when was the last time she was out having fun, dancing and making new acquaintances. And even though it sounded a bit scary, risky and mysterious, she had a good feeling about it, knowing that nothing bad could happen to her with Liam by her side.

Chapter 7

The big day was there. It was eight in the morning and Hayley has just woken up. Normally, she would have stayed in bed till nine as it was Saturday, but today, she was too excited and she had to get up.

- Hi Hayley, you're up? – Isabella called before Hayley even made her bed.

- Yes.

- Good, because we have our hair and nails done at nine- thirty so we need to go.

- OK, are you picking me up?

Isabella hung up and Hayley heard the doorbell. She was already there.

- Give me five minutes, I didn't expect you here so early.

- No worries. First hairdresser then lunch then dresses and we are good to go.

- Wow, you really have it all planned, don't you?

- Of course. This is not my first ball so I know exactly what to do and how much time we need. We will be ready by six.

Hayley quickly put her sweats on and made a messy ponytail without even properly brushing her hair. She petted Lexi goodbye and left in a hurry. She didn't need to worry about the dog as Liam was supposed to pick her up later that morning. He didn't have to go anywhere as his preparation for the ball consisted of taking a shower and putting his suit on so he could take care of Hayley's dog when she was out with his sister.

- How are you feeling Hayley? – asked Isabella as they were already in the car. The roads were a unusually busy that morning so they needed patiently get through the traffic.

- Excited but also a bit nervous.

- Why nervous?

- Well, there will be many vampires there and Liam said that a stronger vampire could kill the weaker one... Do you think there are many vampires stronger than you two?

- None.

- How come? How can you be so sure?

- Because we are the first vampires. I'm surprised you didn't know that. Didn't Liam tell you?

- No. But I have never asked.

- What the hell have you two talked about all that time?

- There was always something to talk about. I asked some questions every now and then but never cared to ask this one. So tell me, how did that happen?

It was an hour drive so they had plenty of time. Isabella couldn't believe she was the one to tell Hayley that story. She was so sure Hayley already knew everything and there were no more unanswered questions left, considering how much time she had spent with Liam over those few months.

- Well, times were difficult. Many people were dying young either because of a disease or fighting. My mother worried about us, our father died fighting and she was heartbroken. She was a witch though not a very good one. She prepared a spell to make us stronger and resistant, but something went wrong and she made us nearly immortal. For something like that there is always a price to pay. She thought it would be her but it was us who would bear the consequences of her actions. We were improved in many ways but we were craving blood. It was our price, a side effect you may say. Mother was terrified, especially when we killed for the first time and the other witches came after us. They said we were an abomination and we should not be an element of nature. My mother protected us and we managed to run away but she was killed. Witches couldn't let her practice that kind of magic, they perceived her as a threat to their community. Anyway, we turned to Leah for help. At first she wanted to give us up to the witches, but we had been friends since we were kids and she couldn't do it. She couldn't believe that we were just all evil. She created a spell to help us control the hunger and she put another spell on us so the other witches couldn't find us with their magic. We were discovering our new selves with Leah's help. She has amended what our mother created, she improved her spell, but she couldn't reverse what our mother has done. She was working hard trying to make us human again but it was impossible. To be reborn as a vampire, we had to die first. But there was no way to die as a vampire and be reborn human again. And there were no other witches we could have asked for help as they were all after us. But after a while they have given up. They couldn't find us with their magic so they assumed we died after all. With years, new vampires appeared and nowadays both kinds are at peace. We managed to coexist. So, coming back to one of your questions, as we are the first of our kind, we are therefore the strongest. That's why I am sure you'll be safe with us as nobody would stand up against me or Liam.

- It's a very sad story. I can't understand though why those witches didn't want to help you? You were obviously lost and scared. They could have come up with a proper solution and help you. And how could they kill one of their own? That's terrible!

- They were afraid of unknown. In their eyes, we were murderers and monsters and they didn't know what to expect... My mother crossed the line with her spell. It was some dark magic that was forbidden in the witch community. My mother broke the rule and needed to be punished. It was different back then and you may not understand it now.

- I'm glad Leah helped you. She obviously was a good friend.

- Yes, she was the best. And she was one of the most gifted witches I have ever heard of. With her, everything that seemed impossible, became possible. There were only a few things that she couldn't do, I really don't know where she got that much power from. Maybe she made a pact with the devil and just failed to mention that to us?

- Well, I guess you'll never know.

They were ready for their first stop. Isabella picked up one of the most expensive salons to get their hair and nails done. Everyone was so nice to them, offering cakes and coffee. There was relaxing music in the background and very intense smell of flowers and fruit. Hayley felt like a princess with a nice warm towel on her face, two ladies massaging her hands and her feet being deep in a warm milky water with rose petals.

- I wish I could spend every day like this. It's so relaxing.

- There are similar salons in Aspen so you don't have to go that far next time. I just picked this one now as it's my favourite. I don't see why you couldn't do this a few times a week. You don't have to wait for a special occasion to make yourself look and feel good, Hayley.

After a couple of hours, they were ready for their next stop - shopping. They parked in front of those ridiculously expensive shops that always seemed to be empty.

- Isabella are you nuts? Who can afford these dresses?

- I can so don't worry about the money, when you live forever you have plenty so it's all on me. I want you to feel special and you deserve the best of the best.

They went inside. A perfect-looking young woman approached them with a smile. *'She looks like a model'* thought Hayley looking at the blond girl in a skin-tight black dress.

- Miss Anderson, welcome. My name is Jennifer.

- Hello Jennifer. This is my friend Hayley. Do you have our dresses ready?

- Of course. Hello Hayley, nice to meet you. Ladies, would you like something to drink?

- Champaign, please. Hayley?

- Nothing for me, thank you.

Hayley was amazed how elegant everything was. She was feeling horrible in there wearing those sweats. Why didn't Isabella tell her anything in the morning? She should not be wearing sweats in a place like that. Hayley felt like a tramp in that store and if she had come there all by herself, they would have thrown her out for sure. She would've been treated like the girl from the Pretty Woman, no doubt.

Isabella had her dress ready and she knew it was perfect so she didn't even have to try it on. Beautiful long red dress that would look perfect with her blond hair. For Hayley, there were a few dresses ready. Isabella was sitting comfortably on a big sofa, drinking her favourite champaign when Hayley was walking in and out of the fitting room, trying on different dresses. It was taking Hayley long time as she was extremely careful with each dress knowing how expensive they were. After over one hour, Isabella finally made her choice.

- This one! Definitely this one. It looks perfect!

Hayley was wearing a slim long golden dress with no back. It was silky smooth, feeling cool on Hayley's skin and it fitted her perfectly. They picked up their masks and hit the road. On their way back home, they made one more stop and Isabella picked up the jewellery set she had ordered for Hayley. It was a necklace and earrings in the same style as Hayley's magical ring.

They were at Liam's at five thirty and everything was as scheduled. Hayley picked up Lexi and took her home. She was supposed to wait for Isabella and Liam to pick her up at six.

At six sharp, Hayley heard the horn - a long black limousine was waiting outside. Hayley took a look in the mirror for the last time and she was so pleased to see that she looked perfect, even unrecognisable.

- You look ravishing, Hayley. – said Liam when she approached the limousine.

- Thank you. You look good too.

That complement made her blush. She gazed at Liam who looked very handsome in his suit. Her heart started beating faster and she felt like a teenage girl sitting next to her celebrity crush.

It was quarter to seven when the limousine finally stopped. Many guests were already there, talking to each other and laughing. Liam took Hayley's hand and they started walking towards the entrance. Everyone was greeting them when they were passing by as everyone knew Liam and Isabella. After that night, they would all know Hayley too. The ballroom looked amazing and Hayley has never seen so much gold in one place - chandeliers, columns, window frames, all in gold, which was very impressive. There was a table section on one side, a small orchestra on the other and an enormous dance floor in the middle. The mirrors on the walls made that place look even bigger. There were many statues all around the ballroom, the kind of statues that could be seen in Rome. There were also many paintings and Hayley wanted to stop and admire all of them. They were huge and breathtaking, presenting landscapes, horses and wild animals. The most fascinating one was a white hart standing in a meadow, surrendered by the morning fog.

Hayley has never seen such an impressive painting before and Liam had to pull her away by the hand so she didn't spend the whole evening staring at it.

- Isabella and Liam Anderson. Good evening. And who's your friend?

A young man approached them when they sat at their table. He must have been in his twenties, looking younger than Hayley and Liam and the lack of beard or moustache made him look a bit boyish.

- Good evening Ethan. I'm glad you could make it. Please, meet Hayley Evans, our dear friend.

Ethan reached for Hayley's hand.

- Good evening Hayley, pleasure to meet you. A friend of Liam's is a friend of mine. I'm Ethan Jones.

- Nice to meet you Ethan. So how you two know each other?

- We were fighting together during the Second World War. I'm glad he was there. If it hadn't been for Liam, I wouldn't be here with you today. How about you?

Hayley thought for a moment before she replied.

- Liam saved my life too.

- Well, looks like we have something in common already. Let me get us all something to drink.

With everything that was going on that day, Hayley has completely forgotten about vampires. She was so focused on her look and appropriate behaviour. She wanted to fit in and she was glad that Isabella made such an effort to make her look so elegant and beautiful. Her little talk with Ethan reminded her where she was and she got a bit anxious. She looked at her ring to make sure it was there. She hoped the magic within would work for the whole evening and there was nothing to worry about.

The host welcomed everyone wishing them a great evening and the music started. Liam asked Hayley for a dance. She felt his hand on her waist, he has never been so close and her heart started beating faster again. They started slowly to swing.

- You look exceptionally beautiful tonight. I'm glad you're here with me.

Hayley blushed. She got used to Liam being around and she loved spending time with him but that night was different. He was holding her tightly in his arms and there was nothing but thin air between them. She enjoyed his close company. Neither of them was a professional dancer but they both liked the way they danced together. They danced for a few minutes and went back to the table. They talked to Isabella and Ethan and had a few laughs. Every now and then, someone approached their table to introduce themselves. They haven't seen Liam around for a while so his appearance that night was very unexpected. Hayley was drawing a lot of attention as his plus one. Many people were looking at her but only a few decided to introduce themselves. After a few more dances, Hayley left the ballroom and decided to take a walk around the building. Liam found her on the balcony, looking at the garden that was beautifully lit up.

- Why won't you come inside? It's getting chilly.

- I'm OK, just a few more minutes. The garden looks so lovely. Someone has put a lot of time and money into it.

- How are you feeling Hayley? Are you having a good time?

- It looks like a dream. This place, these people... I have dreamt about a ball like this since I was a little girl. I remember when my mum read to me about Cinderella. The story seemed so sad at first but then turned into something so beautiful and I was so fascinated by it. The beautiful dress made of gold, dancing with the prince, the ball. And today it all feels like a fairytale. I have my golden dress and everyone is looking at me wondering who I am... It all makes me feel like I'm Cinderella tonight.

- It looks like all you need is a prince.

Hayley looked at Liam smiling.

- I think you are playing your part quite well. I don't need an actual prince, I just need a dancing partner.

- I'm glad I'm enough.

They went inside and sat at the table. Hayley was looking at the dancing couples, wondering if all those beautiful and sophisticated vampires were as good as Liam and Isabella. They represented a higher class and it was hard to believe that any of them could be a blood-thirsty monster like the one that attacked her in October. But she stopped thinking about it the moment she started dancing again. She felt like a princess in Liam's arms and she hoped that night could last forever.

The host announced the last dance and the evening was coming to an end as it was already after midnight. Hayley and Liam were on the dance floor, waiting for the music to start playing. She got an impression that Liam was even closer than before. He looked so charming in his black suit and the mask. After a few minutes, he looked deep into Hayley's eyes and slowly leaned forward to kiss her. Then, he looked at her again and whispered:

- I think I'm falling in love with you.

Suddenly, the music stopped and everyone started clapping, thanking the orchestra and the host for the evening. Hayley took a step back without a word and they both started clapping along with the rest. They collected their stuff and all four were ready to go home. Hayley was quiet through the whole ride. She was thinking about the kiss and what Liam told her. She treated him like a friend and never thought they could be something more. But when he said those words, she realised she had feelings for him as well. All of a sudden, he stopped being just her friend and she wanted to be in his arms again. The limousine stopped outside Hayley's house first.

- Thank you all for an amazing evening. I had a really good time.

She opened the door but didn't come out.

- Liam… would you like to come in for a cup of tea?

- Absolutely – He responded immediately.

They both got out and went inside. Hayley was locking the door behind them when she felt Liam's kisses on her neck. Before she even realised, within a blink of an eye, they were in her bedroom. Liam tore his shirt along with the tie and the buttons shot across the room in all directions. Hayley laughed but then got all serious.

- Do not do that to this dress! It was very expensive.

- I won't. - He smiled.

He gently took her dress off and put it on the chair. They didn't realise how much they wanted each other until that very moment. There was no better way to end that already perfect day.

- Hi Liam, where are you? – said Isabella over the phone, surprised to discover that Liam was not home.

- I am at Hayley's.

- Already? It's eight in the morning... wait... are you already there... or still?

- Still.

- Oh... OK...I'll see you later then.

Liam was still in bed with Hayley when Isabella called. They spent an amazing night together. He was happy and so was she. It was nice to feel loved and wanted again. Their story has just begun and they wanted to enjoy every moment together.

Shortly after noon, Liam left to see Isabella and Hayley took a long, relaxing bath and ordered a takeaway. Liam didn't want to leave but a few hours apart made their evening together even more precious and appreciated.

- All I wanted to say is that I like you Hayley. – said Isabella, showing at Hayley's suddenly and unexpectedly as she tended to do - You are a very good friend to me, so if something goes wrong between you and Liam, could you please promise me that we will still be friends? I don't want that stupid, awkward situation when you two don't talk to each other and I cannot see you anymore.

- Don't worry Isabella, I promise we'll stay friends. The question is, would you still be my friend, once I'm all wrinkled and slow and start forgetting my own name?

- Well, what's the point? If you can't remember your own name, there is a big chance you won't remember mine either.

They both laughed.

- Hayley, have you ever considered becoming a vampire?

Isabella surprised her with that question.

- I have, once or twice. But it scares me.

- And death doesn't scare you?

- Not that much. I would say it interests me. Nobody knows what the next part is, what really happens when you die. Possibly, there is nothing, but what if there is an afterlife and it's amazing? Would I want to miss that for the promise of eternal life on earth? I am not sure.

- Leah, our witch friend, told us that there was an afterlife, she was able to communicate with her ancestors, but maybe it's different for witches. But, if there is something for them, maybe there is also something for humans.

- I like this idea.

- Did Liam talk to you about it?

- No, but I think it's too soon to have such a conversation. We love spending time together and we want it to last. I already know that me and Liam don't have a future together. In ten years, I would look older than him. He would have to move to a different city or country and I would stay here. But I want to enjoy these moments now. I don't know how much time I have left so I don't want to ruin a good time thinking about the future that may never come.

- I can't imagine being human again. Knowing that tomorrow may never come, wondering how much time I have left. It's terrifying and sad.

- You may think so, but it makes me appreciate the time I have now and I don't want to leave anything for tomorrow. I am grateful for every happy moment I have. I don't postpone anything for later if I can enjoy it today.

- I understand you Hayley. I just know that this is not something I would want for myself. Anyway, how about a little adventure? I'm after this one guy who killed a family of five and is still on the loose. I know where he is and I am going to see him tonight. Would you like to see me emotionally torture this guy before I deliver him to the police? Trust me, it's fun.

- Well, it is something I have never experienced before so yeah, count me in.

- Great. I'll pick you up at seven. I'll tell Liam you are unavailable this evening and he doesn't have to wait up.

Isabella picked Hayley up as planned. They didn't travel far, the guy was in a small town nearby, in a Woody Creek Tavern. He was already a bit drunk although it was still an early evening. They didn't wait too long in the car as Isabella wanted him conscious and was afraid he could get too drunk and pass out, taking all the fun away. She went to the pub, laughed a bit with the guy and they left together. They took his car but she offered she would drive. Hayley followed them to a small motel. She waited in the car five minutes, giving Isabella enough time. When she went inside the room, the guy was already tied to a chair and his nose was broken. He was swearing a lot, confused by what was going on. He was not scared, just angry, really angry.

- Who the hell are you?! What do you want from me?!

Isabella didn't answer and just punched him again. Hayley sat on the chair in the dark corner. The guy didn't even notice she was there. It was a man in his fifties, well-built, with short greyish hair and a few days' stubble. He smelled of alcohol and cigarettes and his clothes clearly haven't been washed in a while.

- I am disgusted by people like you, Mr Brown. You killed that poor family for no reason and you think you can just walk way.

- What you care? You knew them?

- No, but I do care after all. I search for people like you to make them pay for what they've done. You see, I can make you cry, Mr Brown.

He laughed.

- I am not afraid of pain. I'm not afraid of you or the police or anyone. I can go to jail, I don't care. I would be a star in prison so go on, do what you want, I dare you.

- You're not afraid of me, you said? Well, I think you should be.

Isabella leaned towards him, her eyes turned black.

- Do you believe in devil, Mr Brown?

The guy started screaming but Isabella put her hand over his mouth.

- Why are you screaming? Are you afraid now?

He nodded. He was clearly terrified.

- I know a few people who can make your life a living hell in any prison cell you would get into. Wherever you go, remember, there is a bigger evil, lurking in the shadows, watching your every step and compared to that darkness, you are nothing. You will see my face in every dark corner for the rest of your miserable, pointless life. And wherever you go, remember I may already be there waiting for you.

And she bit his neck. The guy wanted to scream but she was still covering his mouth. She left a terrible wound and the blood was pouring down his shirt. When she took a step back, he was crying.

- Please, please, I don't know what you are but I'll do anything you want.

- There is no hope for you anymore. I'll wait for you in hell.

She licked his blood off her fingers and punched the guy again but this time she knocked him out. Her face came back to normal.

- So, how did you enjoy the show, Hayley? - she said and started cleaning her face and hands.

- Wow, that was very scary. You are very scary. I'm glad I haven't met you under any other circumstances.

- I love my job. It never gets boring. I see these scumbags thinking they are gods and then I see them crying and peeing themselves in horror. Some things don't change with time. Like faith. People may believe in different gods or believe in nothing at all, but once they see something terrifying that they can't explain, the only word coming to their mind is 'devil'. After something like this, they all believe in devil and it haunts them for the rest of their life. And I love this! I love knowing that they were punished with more than just a prison cell. OK, it's time to get this pathetic creature to the police and get my reward. I will drive him in his car and you can follow so you can give me a ride back home later. It won't take long, I promise. There's only some paperwork to do and I'll be good to go.

Hayley realised what a powerful creature Isabella was. She was her friend but to others, she was a real monster. And so was Liam. They were truly powerful and if they ever turned bad, there would be no hope for humankind. Hayley was truly scared seeing Isabella like that. She was invincible and unstoppable which was what Hayley always longed to be, powerful and fearless. But being a vampire was more than just all the perks. *'What if I killed someone innocent because I couldn't control myself? What if I hurt April or June? Would I be able to live with that?'*

Hayley thought about turning into a vampire before as she envied Isabella and Liam many things. *'It must be an amazing feeling, knowing that nobody could hurt you, that you would never get old or ill. That you are the strongest creature on this planet, truly invincible.'* With the eyes of her imagination she saw herself walking around at night, confident and powerful. She could see Mr Brown trying to run away from her as she was chasing him through the dark streets of the empty and silent city. She could nearly enjoy her new self, nearly taste the power. She thought about becoming a vampire once and she would definitely give it another thought again.

The next day was very busy for Hayley and she has been impatiently watching the clock on the wall waiting for her evening walk with Liam. As she was putting her shoes on, she heard Isabella talking to someone on the driveway. When she opened the door, she noticed that Isabella came over with a friend which was very surprising as Hayley didn't expect her, even less so in a company of a stranger.

- Hayley, this is a friend of mine, Sarah. She's a witch and I asked her to perform a protective spell for you.

Sarah was short but fit. She had incredibly long wavy ginger hair and her eyes were pure emerald. She had a ring on nearly every finger and lots of self-made leather bracelets that made her look a bit hippy and childish.

- Hi Hayley, nice to meet you. - Her voice was warm and soothing - So I thought I could cast a spell on this house so no vampire other than Isabella and Liam could enter unless you invite them in. Would you like that?

- Hi, yes, sure, sounds great. Thank you.

- Great, let me get my stuff ready.

Hayley and Isabella sat at the kitchen table when Sarah was setting up her stuff on the floor. First, she lit a candle. Then, she put some soil into a bowl along with water and herbs and a few drops of Liam's and Isabella's blood that she already had in a small vial. Then, she started chanting in some unknown language. Her eyes were closed and her hands were a few inches above the bowl. The candle extinguished at the same time that all ingredients in the bowl started burning. After a minute, the bowl was full of ashes. Sarah started walking around the house, scattering the ashes and saying aloud some spells. The moment the ashes hit the door, the windows or the floor, they disappeared with a silent hiss, leaving no trace. Hayley has never seen anything like that before. It reminded her of a show that could be seen in Las Vegas or New Orleans. It was a performance that could attract many tourists and yet it was real magic.

- All done, you're safe here. By the way, I like your ring, I can feel its magic. Whoever gave it to you was very powerful. The spell within is very strong.

- Thank you, Sarah. How can I pay you for this?

- Don't worry, Isabella already has. It was a simple service. Here's my card if you ever needed anything. Nice meeting you. Take care.

Sarah took her stuff and left in a hurry. Hayley sat completely motionless, still impressed by the magic she saw.

- Isabella, why did you bring her here? – she asked frowning her brow.

- What do you mean?

- I thought with you as my friends and with that magical ring I am safe already. Why did I need that spell?

- Well, you can never be too sure. There was an opportunity to make you safer and I took it. I thought you would be glad.

- I am glad and I appreciate you did this for me, but now I am a bit scared that I'm in some kind of a danger and there is something you are not telling me. Is there, Isabella?

- No, Hayley, of course not. Don't worry.

- OK, well, thank you for looking after me, I appreciate your effort. You are a good friend.

- I nearly forgot! – said Isabella being halfway from the door - Hayley, would you like to go to Miami with us? We wanted to go last year but then you came along and that topic never came up again, somehow.

- Of course I would! I have never been to Florida but I loved the beaches in California. When are you going?

- This Saturday.

- For how long?

- Three or four days.

- Why didn't you tell me earlier? I have some patients scheduled.

- Well, it was a surprise for us too. Ethan planned it all and wanted to surprise us.

- Ethan? I thought he left Aspen.

- No, he actually decided to move in... We have been seeing each other since the ball.

- Are you two together?

- Kind of. I mean, we have been a couple many times. We just keep breaking up. Now, looks like we are a couple again.

- Why do you keep breaking up?

- I don't know, it's complicated. Life is different when you live as long as we do. It's not just one lifetime, it's a few so your perception is different.

- Right… I need to make a few phone calls and get my appointments rescheduled. I hope my sisters would take care of Lexi. I will come back to you on this later. Hopefully, I will get everything sorted, but next time, you need to give me more notice. I am not a last-minute type anymore.

But even though Hayley was packing in a hurry and nervously trying to have everything well organised before the trip, she was still very happy and excited about the journey. It was a while since she has been anywhere on holidays and she couldn't wait to see Miami and enjoy the heat and the sunshine. She knew she would have much fun, especially in such a great company. She needed some time off. For the past few months, she hasn't really had a moment for herself. Work, Lexi, Liam – she loved all three main aspects of her life but she needed something different at least for a moment. She thought about lying on the beach with no responsibilities, no phone, no watch, where she could enjoy the sound of the ocean, the gentle touch of a cool breeze and the lovely warmth of the sun. She smiled with that mental image in her head and sped up the packing.

Chapter 8

Saturday afternoon, they were all checking into the hotel. The flight was nice and without any unpleasant surprises. The weather was perfect, the sun felt warm on their skin but it was not burning and the sky was flawless. A nice change from a cold and cloudy Aspen. They had only ten minutes to get ready for dinner as the table at the restaurant was already reserved.

It was a five-star hotel. The lobby was impressive and very specious. The rooms were huge, with beautiful ocean view and they looked like one of those rooms reserved for famous people. It didn't mean much to Liam, Isabella or Ethan but Hayley was amazed. She was not a cheapskate but she didn't like spending too much. Every now and then, she liked going out and eating in a fancy restaurant or getting herself something a bit more expensive like Dior perfumes or diamond earrings. But she has never stayed in a five-star hotel before so it made quite an impression on her.

The dinner was delicious and the restaurant was not too crowded so the soft violin music playing in the background could still be enjoyed. Although the food was great, the portions were quite small and Hayley left the table still filling a bit hungry. The place was great for a date, being so elegant and quiet, but it was definitely not recommended to someone who expected a proper fulfilling dinner.

It was too late for a swim in the ocean but they went on the beach for an evening dancing and they had a great time. It was shortly before midnight when a half of the crowd was already gone and the other half was extremely drunk but still trying to keep the rhythm. Hayley went aside and laid down on the sand. She was exhausted but in a good way.

- Look at the stars Liam. The sky looks beautiful.

Liam took Hayley's hand and they laid on the sand together..

- So tell me Liam, how did you meet Ethan?

- It was during the war. I remember as if it was yesterday. There were only five of us in the trenches. The Germans where coming closer and we knew they would never let us out alive. Boys were sitting on the ground, waiting for death. They were looking at the photos of their wives and kids and saying their goodbyes. I suggested I would go and check how many Germans were there and look for a way out. They told me it was a stupid idea but we were about to die anyway so they didn't really care what I wanted to do. And so I went out and I ran quickly to the other trenches. They were about ten Germans in there. I took them by surprise, killing them one by one. Some of them managed to fire a few shots though so when I came back to my guys they looked at me as if I was a ghost. They wanted to know what happened so I told them there were only three Germans in there and I killed them. They noticed wholes in my uniform but didn't ask any questions. They were happy to be alive. The next day, once we started moving forward again, we were fired at and we all got hit. I dragged my guys into the nearest trenches, they were dying. They were begging me to do something and I could see fear and despair in their eyes. You cannot possibly imagine what it's like during the war. When the missiles are flying over your head and you never know when one of them will hit you; when the sky is dark although it's the middle of the day; when the air is full of smoke and it's hard to breathe…. Being in a place like that, even for a short time makes you forget the basic things you enjoyed before like the smell of cut grass or a taste of a fresh bread roll or the softness of the pillow… I was a vampire but even I didn't know if I was to return home safely. One bomb explosion and I was dead, regardless how powerful I was. So… I turned them to give them hope. Ethan was one of them and he is the only one who stayed in touch with me. His wife died during the war and he had nobody else so he joined me and Isabella. He always sticks around for a few years and then he's gone again. He is a good guy and a very good friend too.

- Wow, he's lucky you were there. So how did you discover how to turn other people? Did Leah tell you that?

- No, I turned the first person by accident. It was a few years after me and Isabella were turned. There was this young girl Fiona. She was very poor, living with her mother in a small cottage in the woods. One day, she attacked me with a knife and wanted to rob me. She managed to cut my palm. When I grabbed her by the hand to get the knife, she started to scream so I covered her mouth with my bleeding hand. Then she bit me so I pushed her away but I did it a little too hard. She fell down and hit the back of her head and died instantly. I believe she must have tasted my blood when she bit me, that's why she was turned. I didn't know anything about it back then. I thought I killed her so I left her in the woods. She found me a few days later asking me to explain what happened to her. Apparently, when she came back to life, she went home and accidentally killed her mother. She blamed that on me. She loved her mother but killed her because of the hunger she couldn't control. Fiona has never forgiven me for leaving her in the woods like that. She even tried to kill me a few times before she finally gave up. I haven't seen her in years. I don't know where she is or what her life looks like now. I don't even know if she's still alive.

- That's a really sad story. Poor girl, she must have been terrified.

- I know, but it was an accident. I wanted to help her later, I offered her to join me and Isabella but she was too angry with me, she hated me too much. It still haunts me. I will never forgive myself for that.

- Don't think about it anymore. You can't change your past so just try to enjoy the present.

They stayed on the beach till the sun rise. The view was truly breathtaking as the sky was slowly changing from dark and navy to orange and gold.

- Did you have a good time in the city? - Liam asked seeing Isabella and Ethan coming back to the hotel.

- Yes it was great! - Isabella was very excited and full of energy. - What a night! How about you two? Did you just wake up for the sunrise or did you spend the night on the beach?

- We spent the night here. - Liam responded. - But I think we'll go back to the hotel now, freshen up and have some breakfast.

- Good idea, let's meet here in two hours. Apparently, Amanda and Tom have a surprise for us.

- Who are they? - Hayley asked surprised.

- They are our friends. We haven't seen each other for years. I didn't even know they were here.

- We ran into each other. - Ethan said. - They are here only for a few days.

- Can't wait to see them. You'll like them Hayley, they are a very nice couple. OK, so, this spot in two hours?

- Exactly. See you then.

- Change of plans. – said Ethan storming into Liam and Hayley's hotel room - Amanda and Tom invited us to go sailing with them on their yacht and they are already waiting downstairs. Are you two ready yet?

Before Liam managed to answer, Hayley came out of the bathroom. Ethan looked at her and his face got serious.

Hayley saw the panic on their faces and suddenly realised what it was about. She ran back to the bathroom and quickly put her ring back on but didn't come out. Ethan was shocked.

- How come Hayley is human again? How did that happen? What kind of magic is this?

- She's not human again. Hayley is human. Always was. - Liam said.

- She was a vampire when I met her at the ball and yesterday.

- She was under a spell to give you an impression she was a vampire. We wanted her to go with us and she couldn't have gone as human.

- So Hayley is human?

- Yes Ethan, she is.

- I assume she knows about us?

- She does. It's a long story. But you can trust her Ethan, she's a friend.

Hayley came out of the bathroom but this time she was wearing her ring.

- Well done Hayley, you really amazed me. I thought nothing could surprise me anymore and here you are. One minute you are a vampire and the other you're human.

- Sorry Ethan for confusion. It won't happen again.

- Don't worry my dear, I don't mind. But I think it's safer for you to pretend you are one of us.

- So, a yacht you said?

- Yes! Be ready in five minutes because we won't wait.

The yacht was beautiful. It was small but still big enough for six people. Isabella and Liam met Amanda and Tom nearly twenty years ago when they moved to Florida. They were not close friends but nevertheless it was nice to see some familiar faces.

- This is Hayley Evans, our newest friend. Hayley, this is Amanda and Tom Greene. We used to be neighbours.

Amanda looked like a model. Her brown curly hair was loosely falling on her neck and her brown eyes seemed full of joy. She was tall and slim and looked amazing in her short summer dress that was partially covering the swimming suit underneath. Tom came across as a quiet man, a bit shy. He was not as fit as Amanda and seemed slightly shorter than her but his green eyes made him look friendly and harmless so Hayley liked him right away.

- Nice to meet you Hayley, welcome onboard –said Amanda - I Hope you'll enjoy your time here.

- Thank you and nice to meet you too. Lovely yacht you have here.

- Thank you. It's perfect when you just want to disappear from the whole world for a week or two. We are happy to rent it if you ever want it.

- I will keep that in mind, thank you.

The interior was very elegant but cosy. There were two beige sofas with many colourful cushions. In the middle, there was an elegant coffee table right on a soft and fluffy rug. There was also a bathroom, a bedroom and a small kitchen. It looked like a small house and Hayley couldn't believe it was just a boat. When she was still admiring the yacht, the other five were already in their swimming suits.

- Come on Hayley, are you swimming with us? - asked Tom - If we're lucky, we may see some dolphins

- Sounds great, but what about the sharks?

- What do you care about the sharks?

Hayley realised she should not be worried about sharks if she pretended to be a vampire.

- I just don't like them. So you better be sure there are none there, otherwise I won't get into the water.

- Well, I have never seen any here but let us check.

All five jumped into the ocean. Water was warm and clear. Liam took a deep dive to make sure there were no sharks.

- Come on Hayley! It's safe!

Hayley changed into her swimming suit and made sure the ring was on. She jumped into the water and dived in with Liam. They saw many colourful fish, some swordfish and turtles. Hayley was amazed. She didn't know how big those turtles could get until she has seen them with her own eyes.

- Guys! Look! Dolphins!

Hayley saw a few dolphins swimming their direction. They were jumping above water and making funny noises. She wished she could pet them, they were so close. They seemed bigger than she imagined them.

- That's amazing. Wow!

- Is this your first time swimming with the dolphins? - asked Amanda.

- Yes and I will never forget this. I need to tell my sisters about it. They have to experience this. Wow! Truly amazing!

Dolphins were swimming around them for a couple of minutes. Hayley managed to touch one of them with the tips of her fingers. It was smooth and slick. Once the dolphins have swum away, everyone returned on the deck.

- So Hayley, did you like it? - Amanda asked.

- Yes! It was great.

- Yes it feels great every time and I have seen dolphins like twenty times already.

- I envy you. Looks like you are living a dream.

- Yes, we love the sun and the ocean, so every time we need to move again, we look for beaches and hot weather. We have lived in Miami about twenty years ago. Between now and then, we have lived in Jamaica, Tenerife and LA.

- So what's next on your list?

Amanda thought for a few seconds and then started singing.

- *Aruba, Jamaica...*

Tom joined her right away.

- Oh I want to take you to Bermuda, Bahamas, come on pretty mama...

Amanda and Tom started dancing around. It was a pleasant view as they have been together for so many years and yet, their love was evergreen.

- You don't see so much love around anymore. - she said to Liam sitting by her side.

- That's true. I'm glad to see them so happy.

- And they have the whole eternity to share.

Hayley closed her eyes and took a deep breath, wishing that day never ended. It has been a while since she felt so carefree. She had no watch and no phone. She didn't care what day or time it was. She felt as if the time has stopped and there was no world outside that boat. If her life was about to look like that, she was ready to give up her cosy house and her work to pursue that idyllic eternal life.

The next day was even more exciting. They rented jet skis and were on the beach first thing in the morning. Isabella and Hayley were going slowly, trying to figure out how the equipment worked but Liam and Ethan were long gone racing like crazy.

- Look at these two. Big kids.

- What are you talking about Isabella? If I was not afraid to die I would go racing with them. Looks like so much fun! But I still don't know how to ride this bloody thing.

- I don't need to go extreme. I enjoy just being here. The sun, the ocean. Feels like paradise.

- Well, I don't mind a bit of adrenaline every now and then.

Liam and Ethan passed the girls by, splashing them with water and turned around with big smiles on their faces.

- Liam, I am not quite sure how to use it. Would you mind if I sat with you?

- Not at all.

Hayley climbed Liam's jet ski and put her arms around his waist.

- Go as fast as you can. Just like you did with Ethan. I want to see how it feels.

Liam started going faster and faster and Hayley felt the breeze on her face. The wind started slowly pulling her away so she clung to Liam even more tightly. They jumped and hit the water a few times so Liam started slowing down and turned around. Before Hayley even realised, they were back with Isabella and Ethan.

- So, how was it Hayley?

- Amazing! The feeling is great, Isabella you definitely should try it.

- I didn't know you are such a daredevil, Hayley.

- I am not, but I like to experience something new sometimes. I don't do anything too stupid or reckless. Besides, I knew Liam would be careful. - She looked at him with a smile.

They rode jet skis a bit longer, exploring other beaches. After dinner, Liam and Ethan went surfing as the wind got stronger and the waves got bigger. Isabella and Hayley stayed on the beach, enjoying their drinks and the music. In the evening they came back to the hotel to pack their bags and get ready for their flight back home next morning.

- I hope you had a good time, Hayley.

- Yes I did. Thank you Liam for taking me here. I had real fun. I can't believe now we have to go back home. I will miss the sun and the warmth and the ocean. Next time, we need to come here for longer.

- We will. We can go wherever you want. There are many places worth seeing. We could travel the world.

- I'll think about it. Maybe I can ask my sisters to watch my house and Lexi so I could go travelling with you.

- Any particular places on your mind?

- Well, I have a bucket list.

- What's on it?

- I wanted to go to Rome and see Colosseum but I have already done that. I also wanted to swim in the ocean and now I can tick that one off too. I wanted to learn how to play the guitar and that one is done too. Kind of. I mean, I can play a song or two. I wanted to see a whale but not on one of those useless whale watching trips where you sit in a boat and are lucky to see at least the tip of the tail. I wanted to dive in and see the whale under water. It must be a really breathtaking experience. But I don't know how to organise that. Maybe this is something I can focus on when we get back home... I also wanted to see northern lights. It must be truly fascinating to see the sky so colourful. I am happy like a child when I see a rainbow! Once I saw two rainbows one underneath the other and I was staring at the sky like an idiot. Maybe we can organise a trip to Alaska or Canada to see that?

- Good idea. What else is on your list?

- I wanted to write a book but I have never started one. I have a few ideas in my head but noting solid. Maybe, eventually, I'll come up with something interesting. Maybe I can write about vampires? Base it on my very own experience?

- Why not. I bet it would turn out to be a bestseller.

- I also wanted to see what it's like when gravity is gone. Do you know what I mean? But that experience is still pretty expensive so I'll do this one last.

- Nice list. I can help you with that whale watching and northern lights. We can also think about that Zero-G experience. I will browse the internet to see what our

options are. But that book you would have to write on
your own.

- How about you? Do you have a bucket list?

- Not really. I have done so many things and seen so
many places that I don't think there is anything left for me
to explore anymore.

- I assume there is no point of that list if you live
forever.

- I guess not. But I am happy to help you tick yours.

- Home, sweet home.

Hayley went inside her house and sat on the sofa
completely powerless, throwing her head back and closing
her eyes. They came back shortly before noon, after over
six-hour journey. The airports were busier than ever and
Hayley was sick and tired of the sweating heat and noisy
crowds. All she wanted was to take a nice relaxing bath in
her quiet bathroom, hoping that the annoying tinnitus
would eventually go away. She went to pick up Lexi
before she even unpacked. Her brief visit lasted nearly
three hours as April and June had many questions and
carefully looked at every single photo. They have never
been in Miami so they were genuinely interested in
Hayley's thoughts about the trip. And Hayley didn't mind
talking about it, she had so much fun doing things she has
never done before.

After taking a relaxing bath and eating a decent dinner,
Hayley finally sat down and went through her recent
photos again, selecting the ones she would put on the wall.
She smiled looking at the photo of her and Liam, they
looked good together. '*Maybe I should go around the
world with him* – she thought – *I'm still young and healthy
and travelling wouldn't be a problem. We can have so
much fun together, seeing different parts of the world,
discovering new cultures... Well, new only for me, because*

he has already been everywhere and seen everything. But maybe I can still surprise him with something new, maybe there is still something left for him to discover.' She reached for her laptop and started browsing the internet, looking for whale watching trips. She found the Silver Bank, the breeding area for whales, close to Dominican Republic but it was not recommended in May so she had to wait with that trip till autumn. 'That's a shame, *I really hoped this could be the next thing to tick off on my bucket list.'* Still full of hope and excitement, she started searching for any information about the Northern Lights, but it turned out she needed to wait until winter to make sure she would see them. She had to figure out something else for summer. Maybe she could learn a few more songs to play on the guitar? Or start that book she always wanted to write? Her life was not very interesting before and she couldn't find any inspiration but now she could write about vampires and witches and all the magic she has witnessed. Isabella and Liam had many interesting stories that she could use. *'It's definitely worth giving a go.'* - She thought with a smile. Although it wasn't even eight in the evening yet, Hayley closed her laptop and went to bed, feeling exhausted but genuinely happy.

Chapter 9

Hayley woke up in a speeding car. Her hands were tied and she had a headache. She couldn't remember what has happened and how she got into that car. She blinked rapidly a few times as her vision was a bit blurry. When she looked to her left, she saw a young girl behind the wheel. It was a teenager with a long black hair, very slim and pale. Her nails were awfully bitten and her arms were covered in tattoos.

- You're awake, good – said the girl. She seemed annoyed, even angry.

- Who are you? What's going on?

- I'm here to kill you. Although I am still debating on it.

Hayley couldn't understand what was going on. She was sure she didn't recognise the girl, she couldn't be one of her patients. Hayley was getting more and more anxious now, trying secretly to untie her hands.

- Who are you? - she asked with her breaking voice - What have I done to you?

- You? Nothing, you don't even know me. But Liam does.

Hayley tried to think clear, putting together different pieces of information.

- Fiona?

The girl was genuinely surprised.

- So you do know me after all. What did he tell you about me, huh? I'm surprised he even remembered me after all these years.

- He didn't mean to hurt you, it was an accident and he's truly sorry.

- Accident? He killed me and left me in the woods! Do you have any idea what I have gone through?

Fiona sounded furious and Hayley couldn't find any right words to calm her down.

- I woke up in the woods – she continued - I went home and asked my mother to take care of me. I thought I was ill, I felt weird, everything seemed different, my stomach hurt and my heart was beating like crazy. I was eating and eating but I was still hungry. Before I even realised what happened, my mum was lying dead on the floor and my face was covered in her blood. I killed her! My own mother! And I don't even remember doing that! Do you have any idea how that feels?

Hayley didn't know what to say. She didn't want to make Fiona any angrier. It was clear the girl was still hurt, carrying a lot of anger and blame. She hated Liam as much as she hated herself, it was easy to tell. Hayley realised that trying to put Liam in the best light would just make things worse. The better option would be to start acting like a compassionate friend.

- I'm truly sorry, Fiona. I also lost someone I loved and I know...

- Don't try to convince me that you know what I have gone through because you have no idea. You didn't kill your husband, he died in a car accident and I killed my mother so this is not the same.

It was clear that Fiona knew more about Hayley then she thought. She must have done some research, planned it carefully. It was not a spontaneous decision and Fiona must have been watching Hayley for a while.

- I'm sorry, of course I don't know how you feel. But I can imagine it is worse than what I went through and I feel for you, I really do. But why are you hurting me?

- You see, I wanted to kill Liam for what he's done to me but I realised quickly that it was impossible. He was far too strong for me to hurt him in any way so I gave up and tried just to live my life but I couldn't, I couldn't just forgive and forget. I've searched for him many times but he moved around often, leaving nobody and nothing behind, no clues. But one day, I realised the only way to hurt Liam, is by hurting someone he cared about. But every time I finally found him, there was nobody special in his life, only him and Isabella, all these years. So can you imagine my surprise when I saw him with you? Day after day. It was obvious he was happy and I hated it! So I went to your house but I couldn't get in. As I was watching you through the window, once, I saw how you cut yourself with a knife and the wound didn't heal. I couldn't understand how that was possible but then I thought, there must have been some magic involved. I couldn't get inside your house and you were clearly human but something made me think you were a vampire. I decided to stay away, watch you, study you and find out as much as I could. I was thinking how to kill you and I thought how dramatic it would be if you died in a car accident just like your husband.

Hayley felt like crying. The girl sounded very determined and it was clear that there was nothing more important than revenge and she would stop at nothing until she got what she wanted.

- I don't deserve to die like this, Fiona, I have done nothing wrong. If you want to hurt Liam, I can hurt him by leaving him.

- No, it wouldn't be enough. I made up my mind.

Hayley couldn't believe it was the end and she was about to die. She hoped she had at least another thirty years in front of her. Suddenly, she regretted not turning into a vampire earlier. She could have turned and moved in with Liam or travelled around the world with him, living a happy eternal life with a man she loved so much. But Fiona was so motivated to hurt Liam that she didn't care about any collateral damage. Hayley started to cry feeling completely hopeless.

- I am very sorry Hayley, you seem nice and I know you don't deserve it.

- Please... Don't do this. Let's think this through.

- I have thought this through long enough and there is no other way. I will make it quick, you won't feel a thing, I promise. It's better than growing old or dying of a long-term illness. I'm doing you a favour by finishing your life before it started to be unbearable.

Fiona stepped on the pedal and the car started running faster. Hayley closed her eyes right before they hit the tree.

Liam called Hayley a few times but she did not pick up. He was not one of those people who thought 'someone didn't pick up so something bad must have happened' but he had a terrible feeling something was not right. He decided to visit Hayley, just to make sure she was OK. When he got to her house, her car was gone and she was not home. He opened the door using his spare key and decided to wait there for her. After a few minutes he started falling asleep sitting on the couch when his phone rang. He didn't recognise the number.

- Hallo?

- Liam?

- Yes, who is this?

- Liam, this is April, Hayley's sister... Could you please come over to the hospital? Hayley was in an accident.

- I'm on my way.

Liam ran to his house and got into his car, trying to get to the hospital as fast as possible. April sounded very nervous and sad so he knew it must have been something more than just a broken leg. He tried hard not to go through the worst scenarios so he did the best he could to stay focused on driving. When he finally got to the hospital, he saw April and June talking to the doctor on the hall. He approached them quickly, his heart was beating fast and he felt dizzy and sick which has not happened to him since he had stopped being human.

- As I was saying, the patient is stable – the doctor continued - We managed to operate her broken back and although it looks very promising, it's possible she might be paralysed. She has a broken nose, left arm and a few broken ribs but no internal bleeding that could put her life in danger now. She hit her head and is now in coma. At this point, we cannot tell you when she will wake up or what she will remember. It's hard to say how much her brain had been damaged. I'm really sorry I can't give you any more details.

Liam turned around and saw Hayley lying on the bed with a pipe coming out of her mouth. Her face was terribly bruised, her nose was broken.

- I can't believe this is happening. It can't be real, this is not real!

April couldn't catch her breath. June was hugging her, trying to calm her down but she herself was not any less nervous.

- Don't worry, she will wake up. With a good physio, she'll be walking in no time, you'll see. It's going to be OK, April, I'm sure of it.

- Do you know what's happened? – asked Liam with his breaking voice.

- It was a car accident – June said - that's all the police have told us. I don't know who else was in the car. I don't even know if Lexi was there too.

- Lexi is fine, she's home. Could you please take care of her?

- Sure, yes, I will pick her up and take her to our place. Come on April, let's go home, there's no point to be here…

- No, I want to stay. I don't want her to be alone when she wakes up.

- I'll be here – Liam said - I can stay the whole night so you two can go back home. We can take turns if you want just to make sure someone's here when she's awake.

- Thank you Liam. But please, call us immediately if something changes or if the doctor tells you something more, OK?

- Of course, I will. And thank you for calling me.

When the twins left, Liam took a deep breath, went into the room and sat on the chair by the bed. He was looking at Hayley, listening to the machine beeping and pumping oxygen. He gently took Hayley's hand and tears came to his eyes. He reached for his cell phone and called Isabella, telling her all he knew.

- I need you to use all your contacts to find out what's really happened, sister. I won't believe that Hayley has done this to herself, she's too smart for that. There is someone to blame and I want to know who.

- I will do my best and call you soon. Don't worry brother, she'll be fine. She's a tough girl. Everything is going to be OK.

- I don't worry. If she doesn't wake up soon, I will take her out of here.

- Please, don't do anything stupid. Let the doctors do their part.

Isabella worried that Liam would turn Hayley into a vampire out of fear, not giving her a chance to recover in a hospital. A decision like that should be made by that person only and her and Liam exactly knew what it felt like when that decision was made by someone else and they didn't even have a chance to say 'no'. But Liam was too angry and too sad to think clear. As he was sitting by

Hayley's bed, he was planning on how to get her out of the hospital without anyone noticing. He decided he would turn her. He couldn't lose her, not like that, not now when he was finally truly happy.

Three hours later, Isabella came to the hospital. She looked at Hayley and tears came to her eyes. The view was even more heartbreaking than she imagined.

- I'm so sorry, brother.

- Do you have anything for me?

- Yes, right – Isabella wiped the tears from her face and handed Liam the documents. - Hayley was not driving her car. We have a few photos from the cameras showing who was behind the wheel.

Liam looked at the photos terrified, shocked and angry.

- I can't believe it. It's Fiona. I thought she was long gone.

- I know, I thought that too. So you can see that she was driving and Hayley seems to be sleeping next to her. She was obviously unconscious. The police can't identify the driver yet and they think there was someone else involved as someone took the body of the driver. Well, we both know there was no body in the first place and Fiona has probably just got out of that car by herself right before it hit the tree... or right after. A car crash is not something that would kill her so I'm guessing there was nobody else involved.

- She may come back here anytime. If she finds out Hayley has survived the accident, she may come here to finish what she started. It's obvious she wants Hayley dead.

- But why would she hurt her?

- To get her revenge. She knows she can't kill me but Hayley was vulnerable.

- You can't leave this room, Liam. Any nurse or doctor coming over and trying to take Hayley out, you follow them. Don't get her out of your sight. You can trust no one.

- I won't. I won't let anything happen to her again.

- But like I told you over the phone brother, don't do anything stupid. I had my conversation with Hayley about turning and she didn't want that. This is her life Liam, you can't turn her just for yourself, it has to be her decision. Give her some time. She's stable now and she's not in danger anymore so let the humans do their job. She will wake up, I'm sure of it. Have some faith.

Isabella was right. It would be very selfish of him to turn Hayley without her consent.

- Do what you do best and find her, Isabella. And I want her alive, we need to talk before she pays for what she's done.

- I will brother, I will.

Isabella gently kissed Hayley's bruised forehead and left the room. She was furious and very determined to find Fiona. She would make her suffer for what she has done.

Liam was standing by the window, looking down at the busy street. He forgot how fragile people were. There were endless ways to kill but only a few good ways to save a life. He knew Hayley was in good hands and that the doctors wouldn't give up easily. But what's next? Another accident? Illness? What other danger was ahead? He didn't want Hayley to become a vampire, having in mind how much he hated that life himself, but now, when she was a step away from dying, he regretted not discussing that possibility with her. Maybe a life of a vampire seemed so unbearable for him only because he felt lonely, but with Hayley by his side, the eternity didn't seem so bad anymore. It worked perfectly for Isabella and Ethan and also Amanda and Tom.

He sat down by the bed and stroke Hayley's hand.

- I've made a mistake – he said even though she couldn't hear him – We should have talked about it properly, I should have given you a chance to consider that possibility. We could be so happy together, I'm sure of it. There is so much I still don't know about you, so many places I wanted to show you, so many amazing stories I wanted to share… I thought I would never run out of time and here I am, aware that I may not have any more time for all those things I wanted to do with you. The time is taking you away from me and for the first time I hear the clock ticking and it annoys me that we are wasting our precious time together on this! I love you Hayley, I love you so much and even though my heart has been broken many times in the past, I have never suffered as much as I am suffering now, seeing you like this. You said once that you feel safe with me because I can protect you from any danger but I didn't protect you from this. And the truth is that you were in that accident because of me, because I care about you and you were brave enough to care about me…. Maybe not brave but stupid – he smiled through the tears – you are such an idiot to love me, Hayley.

Before he burst into tears even more, his cell phone stared to ring. He reached for it instantly.

- Liam, I found her. – said Isabella - She's with me now at my place. Are you coming?

- Not yet. June will be free to watch Hayley in one hour and we don't want her to be alone when she wakes up so I need to stay a bit longer.

- Of course, I understand. Don't worry, Fiona is not going anywhere, take your time and I will keep here busy until you get here.

Isabella finished her call with Liam and came back to the basement where Fiona was tied to the metal chair with many different chains and ropes. Fiona was strong and could get out of these eventually, but she needed time and Isabella didn't intend to give it to her.

- What have you done, stupid girl? Are you suicidal? You got yourself a death sentence now, you know that? What the hell where you thinking?

- I needed to see him suffer. And now he suffers.

- Hayley is alive. She will walk out of that hospital soon. You achieved nothing, just made Liam angry.

Fiona got upset. She was sure Hayley was in a critical condition, that's what she heard on the news.

- You're lying. She'll die.

- Hayley woke up this morning and is stable. She has a few broken bones and a big bump on her head, that's all.

Before Fiona reacted to that information, Isabella hit her in the face. A few drops of blood fell on the floor before Fiona healed.

- This is going to be the longest and most painful one hour of your life, Fiona, I'll make sure of it.

Liam came over as soon as he could. He went straight to the basement and looked at Fiona with anger, hatred and disgust.

- Isabella, I need you to leave me alone with Fiona now.

- Of course, she's all yours. I will go to check up on Hayley.

Liam heard the car engine and waited for Isabella to drive away. Then, he slowly approached Fiona, trying to stay in control..

- What I have done to you was terrible and unforgivable but it was an accident. I didn't mean to hurt you. But what you did yesterday was well planned and intentional. Hayley has never done anything to you. She is a good person, very compassionate and warm. She could have helped you with your anger and grief. But you just decided to kill her out of spite, just because you were angry with me. I will never let you get away with this... I thought what I would do to you to make you pay, I imagined different terrible scenarios of how I could make you suffer. I see Isabella has already done her part... Even though you're all healed, I know the blood on the floor is yours. I know Isabella long enough to know that she made a good use of that one hour alone with you that I gave her... So I was thinking what else I could possibly do to you, but at the end, I decided I will not be a monster and I won't torture you. Hayley wouldn't want me to. So I will just kill you quickly to make sure you will never hurt her again. I think death would be a just punishment.

Before Fiona said her last words, Liam ripped her heart out and she turned into ashes immediately. He stood there for a few minutes, completely numb. He blamed himself for what has happened to Hayley. '*Would she ever forgive me? Would she leave me? Would she ever wake up or just die in that hospital?*' Thoughts were running through his head and tears filled his eyes. He decided to go back to the hospital before he'd completely fall apart.

Chapter 10

Days and weeks were passing by but Hayley was still in a coma. Her wounds have all healed but her mind was still in the same state as it was the day of the accident. Liam spent every day and night by her bed. The twins were coming over every day so Liam could go home, freshen up and eat. They read news to Hayley, played her favourite music and movies, hoping she could hear them and it would bring her comfort.

It was August, three months later, at the dawn, when Hayley finally opened her eyes.

- Hayley? – Liam quickly approached the bed and leaned forward - Hayley, can you hear me? Do you see me? Say something... Nurse! Nurse! Here! Quickly!

Nurse came along with the doctor nearly instantly They approached Hayley who was lying still, just looking around the room without a word.

- Miss Evans? If you hear me, please squeeze my hand.

Hayley looked at the doctor but didn't squeeze his hand. The doctor was a young man with only a few years of experience working in a hospital. He was tall and slim with short black hair. Lack of any facial hair made him look probably even younger than he truly was.

- Can you talk? Can you tell me your name?

- Hayley – she whispered.

- That's correct. Hayley, you are in a hospital. The car you were driving hit the tree. You broke your back but we operated you immediately and managed to save your spine from further damage. You were in a coma for three months but we believe your life is no longer in danger. Do you remember anything from the day of the accident?

Hayley was lying in her bed still trying to understand what has happened to her. It all felt so unreal. She couldn't remember where she was before she got to the hospital. Fear and shock gradually accelerated her heartbeat, which was reflected by a nearby monitor in a loud beep.

- Three months? – she whispered.

- Yes, Miss Evans. Today is the twenty-eighth of August. Now, please follow my finger.

The doctor did a few tests, asked Hayley to count to ten and backwards and to name all days of the week. He touched her feet but she didn't react to that.

- Hayley, could you please squeeze my hand?

But Hayley didn't move.

- Can you feel my hand in yours?

- No. – Hayley answered confused.

- I will run a few more tests and see what we can do.

The doctor and the nurse left the room leaving Liam alone with Hayley.

- How are you feeling? – Liam sat down on her bed.

Hayley looked at him, sad and scared.

- I feel like I have no muscles and I can't get up. I can't move, I feel numb.

- Is there anything I can get you? Would you like me to call your sisters?

- Not yet, I can't talk to them now. We will call them later, I'm too tired… I'm so tired, Liam…

Hayley started falling asleep again. Liam called the tweens to let them know that Hayley was no longer in a coma and asked them to come over later. He came back to the room, sat by Hayley's bed and held her hand. He was happy she woke up and she remembered him but he was afraid of what would come next as the nearest future did not look bright. The sadness and fear which he saw in her eyes were making even his heart beat faster.

Hayley woke up again shortly after midnight, having slept continuously another fifteen hours. Her sisters visited earlier that day and went back home but Liam was still sitting by her bed.

- Should I call the doctor? Do you need anything?

- It's all coming back to me now... I remember the accident... It was Fiona.

- I know. I'm so sorry, Hayley, it's all my fault.

- No, don't say that, it's not your fault. You didn't know she would go after me so don't blame yourself for what she's done... Do you know where she is now?

- Dead.

- Did you kill her?

- Yes. We couldn't let her hurt you again.

Hayley thought for a minute before she replied.

- I'm glad she's dead, I didn't deserve what she's done to me. I tried talking her out of it but she didn't want to listen. She was evil and it's good that she's gone now. Liam... I see you are holding my hand but I can't feel it. Am I paralysed?

Hayley started crying having realised the condition she was in.

- Please get me out of here – she said with broken words, sounding like a child - I want to go home.

- I'll see what I can do. But I think you should stay here for observation and...

- I don't want to be here. I want to go home, please.

- Go back to sleep now. I will talk to your doctor in the morning.

He kissed her forehead and stroke her head to calm her down. Hayley cried for a few more minutes, not saying anything and then drifted away with the tears running down her cheeks. In the morning, Liam convinced the doctor that he would take Hayley home and provide her with the best private care. The doctor ran a few more tests to make sure there was no internal bleeding or any further damage to the brain. He was not pleased with the fact that his patient would be released so soon after waking up from a coma but there was nothing he could do to stop Liam from taking Hayley away.

- Hayley, I'm sorry we didn't manage to save your spine. The best option would be to try again. I suggest you undergo another surgery and...

- No, doctor, I don't want to be here any longer. You can't help me anymore.

- There is still hope. Please give me a call if you change your mind. I will now prepare the medicine for you along with the information how to take it.

- Thank you doctor, I appreciate your help. I'm sure you've done everything you could and I'm grateful for saving my life.

Doctor gave Hayley a look full of sympathy and left knowing there was nothing more he could say to make her feel any better.

Later that afternoon, Hayley was ready to go home. Liam helped her get dressed and she left the hospital in a wheelchair and with a drip. She was quiet all the way home, lost deep in thought. Isabella, Ethan, April and June were all already there, waiting for her. They also brought Lexi to cheer Hayley up.

- Lexi! My poor dog, I missed you so much! Do you remember me? Did you miss me?

Lexi was so happy to see Hayley. She was barking and jumping around and that made Hayley smile only for a moment though, before she was saddened again by the fact she couldn't pet her dog. Before she burst into tears, Liam took her to the bedroom. He put the wheelchair close to the bed and gently reconnected the drip. April and June exchanged just a few words with Hayley and went back home. They didn't know how to talk to her, unable to find any right words. How could they say that everything would be OK? They didn't know that. Asking her to stay positive and not to worry didn't sound right either. Hayley was in a terrible situation and the only thing they could do was to assure her they loved her and cared for her very much. Their lack of hope was clearly written on their faces and they couldn't hide it behind fake smiles. Liam walked them to the door, ensuring them he would not leave Hayley alone so they didn't have to worry.

- I will stay with you as long as you need me. - said Liam when he came back to Hayley's bedroom - I will look for the best surgeons now and we'll get you to the best hospital first thing tomorrow morning. You will be walking in no time, you'll see. Everything is going to be OK. I will help you, just tell me what you need.

Hayley looked at him with tears in her eyes. It was a look of a person who decided to give up.

- Liam, I was thinking a lot for these past two days and... I can't do it. I can't face it.

- What are you talking about? - Liam sat by the bed and wiped the tears from Hayley's face.

- My body is broken... And so is my spirit. Maybe if I had no other choice, I would gather all my inner strength and look for the best surgeons and try everything but... But knowing there is another way makes me want to choose differently... I can't live like this. I don't want to live like this. I can't... - she turned her face away and let a few teardrops fall on the pillow.

Liam slowly realised what she meant and he didn't know what to think about it. There were pros and cons of what she wanted to do. A day before, he wanted to make that decision for her and now he wasn't sure if it was the right choice.

- Hayley, I think you want this only because you are scared of what's ahead and...

- Of course I'm scared! - she said looking at him again - This was the second time I thought I was going to die and I don't want to feel that way ever again, it moved me to the bone. When I was in that car, I regretted not making that decision sooner.... I just... I can't live like this. It already feels like hell and I know I won't be able to get through it... I can't go on living like this, I'm not strong enough. Please, Liam… help me.

Liam was sitting on Hayley's bed, holding her hand, thinking what to say. Without a word, he just got up and added an extra bag to the drip. Hayley immediately started feeling tired and sleepy again.

- Get some sleep now – he said - We'll come back to this in the morning.

Before Hayley replied to that, she was already asleep.

- How is she? - Isabella sounded sad and worried.

- I did it, Isabella. She asked me to turn her, so I did.

Liam sat at the kitchen table next to his sister.

- It was the right decision Liam. That's what she wants right now, she asked you for it. She knows what she is getting into, she has all the answers and us to help her along the way. She'll be fine, don't worry... Isn't that what you wanted anyway?

- It is... I just hope she won't regret it.

- She was in a terrible state both physically and mentally and she asked for your help. Maybe being a vampire is not a picnic but being nailed to bed sounds even worse. Despite being a great psychologist, she was not strong enough to face such a horrifying future. I'm sure you did the right thing helping her, brother. You put her out of her misery.

- I hope you're right.

Liam went back to Hayley's bedroom, removed the wheelchair and the drip and everything else they brought from the hospital. He kissed Hayley's forehead and left the room.

Hayley woke up ten minutes later. She looked around the room, everything looked normal. Lexi was sleeping by the bed, there was no wheelchair, no drip. She sat on the bed without any difficulties. Nothing hurt her, she felt perfect. She got up slowly and made a few steps. At first, she was confused but then realised it all must have been a bad dream. There was no accident. Nothing happened. She breathed a sigh of relief and smiled. She petted Lexi and hugged her tightly, happy to have her in her arms again. She went to the kitchen and saw Isabella and Liam at the table.

- Hi guys, what are you doing here? What time is it?

- We are waiting for you. How are you feeling?

- Good. Although I had a terrible nightmare. It felt so real though and I still cannot shake it off.

- Hayley, do you remember what we talked about before you fell asleep? - asked Liam suspiciously.

- No, I only remember that bloody nightmare. What did we talk about?

- Hayley, there was no nightmare. Everything you remember really happened... You asked me to turn you, do you remember that? I did what you asked of me.

Hayley sat down, shocked and confused.

- I don't understand... Even if that was true... You said a person needed to die in order to become a vampire and I don't remember dying, I... I didn't die, I'm sure of it. I remember talking to you and then I went to sleep and now I'm here.

- I put morphine into your drip, Hayley. When you drifted away, I gave you a drop of my blood and much more morphine than your body could bear. Your heart stopped for a few minutes... You're in transition, Hayley.

- But... I don't feel any different. I mean... nothing hurts me and I feel OK but...I mean... I feel normal. I'm fine.

Isabella took Hayley by the hand and led her to the mirror in the hallway. Hayley looked at her reflection, her eyes were black and dark veins covered her lower eyelids and upper part of her cheeks.

- Oh my god – she whispered.

- Don't worry Hayley, we're here to help you. Everything is going to be OK – Isabella smiled at Hayley's reflection in the mirror.

- Why do I look like this?

- Because you're hungry. Your face will go back to normal once you've fed. We put some stuff into your fridge. It's more than enough.

Hayley started breathing heavily. Her heart was beating fast.

- It can't be true. This is not happening.

Liam tried to hug her but she stepped back.

- I think I'd like to be alone now. I need to process it... I... Please, go.

- But if you need anything, call me, OK? - Liam sounded very concerned.

Hayley nodded without a word. Liam hesitated but then decided to go, leaving Hayley all alone with her new self, shocked, sad and terrified. She sat on the floor, leaning against the couch, with Lexi by her side.

- What have I done, Lexi? Liam was right, I made that decision because I was weak and scared… I haven't thought that through long enough… What am I going to do now? What am I going to tell my sisters? And what if I hurt someone like Isabella and Liam did? What if I killed April or June like Fiona killed her mother?

Hayley started to cry having realised it was a mistake and there was no turning back. Suddenly, she heard a car parking in front of her house. When she realised it was

Isabella, she felt happy and relieved. She should've never asked them to leave when it was clear she needed their help. She approached the door with her vampire speed and it shocked her a lot.

- Wow – she said to herself before she opened the door – that was cool.

- You didn't think I was really going to leave you alone, did you? - said Isabella passing Hayley by and heading straight to the living room - That was the worst decision of all. You can't be alone now, you'd go crazy!

- I admit, I already started. I'm so glad you're here.

Hayley put her arms around Isabella's neck without thinking and squeezed her so tightly that if Isabella hadn't been a vampire herself, she would have broken.

- Hayley, do you remember Sarah?

- Of course. Hi, nice to see you again.

Sarah looked exactly how Hayley remembered her. Her unusual appearance was nearly screaming 'I'm a witch'.

- Hello Hayley. I heard what has happened and I'm really sorry. But don't worry, I'm here to help.

- Help? What do you mean? – Hayley furrowed her brow.

- I will help you control the hunger just like Leah helped Isabella and Liam back then.

They all sat down in the living room. Sarah put her hands on Hayley's head and closed her eyes. She took a deep breath and started chanting in an unknown language. Hayley didn't feel anything. She expected she would feel something or see something, some proof of magic but there was nothing. All of a sudden, she realised how much she wanted Sarah's blood. Her pulsing veins were within reach, her fingers felt very warm on Hayley's head and her heart was beating so loud she could nearly feel it like the drums during a rock concert. She was struggling to restrain herself from attacking when suddenly the urge stopped, it disappeared completely and she didn't feel hungry anymore.

- All done. – said Sarah with a smile - It should stop you from turning every time you smell, see or want blood.

Isabella handed Hayley a small pocket mirror. She looked into it and smiled seeing her eyes were green again.

- Also, I thought about putting the protection spell on your house again but…

- Again? What happened to the previous one? Why did it stop working?

- Because it was directly linked to you, it disappeared the moment you died.

Hayley looked at Sarah shocked. She knew her heart stopped beating for a few minutes, Liam told her that. But hearing that again from Sarah was still hard to process.

- Hayley, are you OK? I thought you knew how the process worked.

- I know. It's just that… I find it hard to believe… difficult to understand.

- That makes sense. Well, anyway, about that spell, so I thought instead of putting a spell on the house which you would have to leave anyway at some point, I thought I would put the spell on this statue.

Sarah took the statue out of her bag. It was a standing stalion made of bronze. It wasn't big but still quite heavy.

- You don't have to put it anywhere if you don't like it. The magic will still work even if you keep it hidden in a box.

- Sarah that's very kind of you, thank you. I love it, it's very beautiful.

Hayley took the statue and started looking around the living room, trying to find a good spot for it. She decided to put it right next to the TV.

- Great. I'm glad you like it. Anyway, I'll be going now. I have some other work to do. If you ever need me, call me. I'd be happy to help. Take care of yourself and good-bye.

The witch left in a hurry just like last time. *'What a busy little witch'* – Hayley thought – *I bet this is her full-time job and she can make a living from it. I wonder if there is some special job search for witches, some website where they can advertise their services.'*

- Looks like it was a good idea to come back here. You're not ready to be left alone yet Hayley. - Isabella knew that Hayley was crying, it was easy to tell as her eyes were still red.

- Yes, you're absolutely right. I was thinking too much and panicked.

- So what is it that makes you feel so sad? I understand you may be scared because it's all new and unknown but why does it make you sad?

- I'm not sure… Maybe the fact that my entire life is now going to change and I feel not ready for it... I don't know.

- Hayley, your life will change but you can accept those changes because of all these benefits that come with it. You are now strong and invincible and you don't have to worry about getting hurt. You don't need Lexi to protect you anymore, now, you can handle anyone yourself. You are safe in time and don't have to worry about getting old or sick. You have so many possibilities now, you can live wherever you want or sail the world like Amanda and Tom. You are free now. And thanks to Sarah, you don't have to worry you would kill someone accidentally because you have control over it. You also have me and Liam and you can count on us any time. Hayley, it was a good decision, trust me. You would make it sooner or later anyway. Everything is going to be OK.

- What about my sisters? What am I going to tell them?

- Well, you will leave for a few weeks or months now. You'll tell your sisters you are going to see some doctors, that there is still hope for you. Then, you'll come back and live your life normally. We'll figure something out when we have to. You still have plenty of time before you have to leave this town so don't worry about it now.

Hayley started seeing the bright side of her new life and it was less scary now. And knowing that Isabella and Liam went through the same difficult stages, made things a bit easier for her.

- Tomorrow, I will take you out so you can work on your senses.

- Senses? What do you mean?

- Well, you can't really feel any difference now because it's late at night and quiet but tomorrow, you'll see how good your senses are. I'll take you to the woods as the city may be too overwhelming. It will be fine, you are not alone so don't worry. We can answer any questions you may have and we will always be there to help you. It's like… you're a superman now. Do you remember Clark Kent when he was slowly discovering his abilities? He was scared and hated the fact he was different. But then he embraced his true self and learnt to live among people and this is exactly what you are going to do now.

- I like the way you put it, Isabella. – said Hayley with a gentle smile - You make it look so simple now.

- Well, it may not be simple but you will get there eventually. Just try to enjoy your new life because there is no turning back now.

Hayley felt better after her conversation with Isabella. She was still scared but no more sad. Isabella was right. There was no turning back, it was a one-way street that she needed to follow. She locked the door behind Isabella and went to the kitchen. She opened the fridge and looked at its content. The bags were put on a top shelf between tomatoes and a cucumber. It was the most bizarre view Hayley could ever imagine to be real one day.

- OK... Let's do this.

Liam was at Hayley's at seven the next day as he was the one to take her out instead of Isabella. It was bitter-sweet for him to see Hayley as a vampire. He was happy she was safer now and tough and more than able to take care of herself. The passing time was not an issue anymore and they could enjoy each other's company for eternity now. But on the other hand, he knew it was going to be difficult for Hayley to continue to live her regular life, with her job and her sisters living around the corner. Her new diet was not going to be an easy one too and he knew it would be a problem.

Hayley opened the door before he even knocked. She heard him outside, even before Lexi realised someone was at the door.

- Liam, hi. I thought Isabella would take me to the woods today.

- She was going to but I said I would do it. We haven't had a chance to spend much time together since you woke up and I just wanted to make sure you're OK. So pack whatever you want and let's go.

They went to the same woods they chose for hiking a few months before. There was nobody there so they could talk freely and be completely honest with each other.

- So, how are you feeling?

- I'm OK. I didn't sleep at all last night though as my neighbour was snoring. I haven't heard that before but now, it was very loud and kept me awake. I don't feel tired though which is good. In the past, I couldn't get through the day even if I slept only one hour less than usual. Now, I can go on without a single minute of sleep feeling absolutely fine. I like that. – She added with a smile.

- You'll get used to that. With time, you'll learn to ignore some sounds just like you would as human.

They walked for a couple of minutes in silence. Liam didn't want to ask all the questions, he wanted Hayley to talk to him, to tell him exactly how she felt and what she thought.

- Wow, I thought these woods were so quiet but now I can hear all these birds so loud and clear... and the squirls and mice… How can I ever get used to that?

- Don't worry, you'll be fine. Give it a week or two.

They were walking fast and Hayley loved it that she was not feeling tired at all. She enjoyed her time with Liam. Although their walk started with making sure she was OK, now they talked and laughed as if nothing has changed, covering the same topics as usual.

- Stop for a second Hayley and tell me, what do you smell?

Hayley closed her eyes and took a deep breath.

- So many different things I can't even name them all.

- Which smell is the strongest?

- I would say – she sniffed again - something that reminds me of a dog?

- Correct. That would be a wolf.

- There's a wolf here?

- Not too far away. Come on, let's see it.

They walked quickly among the trees, getting farther and farther away from the path. Hayley had to push back the branches so they didn't hit her in the face. Suddenly, Liam stopped and then started sneaking quietly, Hayley followed him the same way. They found a large grey wolf by the river. It was drinking water, not paying any attention to Hayley or Liam.

- Go on, get closer. It won't hurt you.

The noise of the river drowned out their whispers.

- Are you sure?

- Trust me.

Hayley made a few steps towards the wolf. When the stick lying on the ground broke under her shoe, the animal turned around and looked at her. For a moment, it was just standing there, looking into Hayley's eyes and sniffing. Then, it growled quietly and started walking away.

- That was amazing! Wow! Did you see that? Why didn't it attack? I was so sure it was about to start chasing me.

- Because it could tell you were the stronger one. It could sense it, somehow. If you had made a step closer, it would have probably attacked you to protect itself... or would have run away to save itself, I don't know. I'm no expert.

- Amazing feeling looking into wolf's eyes like that. It was a wild animal and there were no fences between us and it was right in front of me, nearly within my reach. What else can I do? Can I fly?

- You wish! - Liam laughed.

- Can I jump super high, like in the movies?

- Not more than you could before, I'm afraid. I'm sorry to disappoint you Hayley. It looks like you expected a bit more than you actually got.

- No Liam, don't get me wrong, I am just checking if there is anything I don't know yet.

- I don't think so. You can't jump high but you can jump from a height and you'd be fine. Maybe we can find some high cliffs for you to jump off so you can get a thrill.

- Sounds good. I would also like to skydive. I always wanted to but I was too afraid to do it. But now that I know I would be safe, I would like to try that.

- We will. Now, you can do whatever you want, Hayley. And you have plenty of time so you can try everything and I am happy to try it all with you.

He brushed her hair away from her face and kissed her. They were standing by the river with nobody around and were truly happy. Now, knowing that Hayley was no longer vulnerable and her mortality was no longer in their way, Liam could clearly picture their life together. She was everything he ever wanted and he knew she loved him too, he could see it in her eyes.

- I love you Hayley. I loved you before and I love you now. You are still the same wonderful person to me whether you are a human or a vampire... or a mermaid.

Hayley laughed.

- Do mermaids exist? Have you seen one?

- No, Hayley, there is no such thing as a mermaid.

- What a pity, I really wanted to meet one. Liam, I love you too. At first I was afraid we would have to break up at some point and what we had was only temporary, but now, I see no reason why we could not spend the eternity together.

Liam smiled, reached to his pocket and got on his knee. Even though he's done it a couple of times in the past, his heart was still beating fast and his mouth got dry, being as nervous as if it was his first proposal.

- Hayley Evens, will you marry me?

The ring was beautiful. No huge diamonds, just a sapphire stone with a silver band. Very simple and classy.

- I know how much you liked the other ring so I thought...

- It's beautiful Liam, I love it. Besides, it doesn't matter what ring you have for me. With no ring at all, my answer would still be 'yes.'

Liam put the ring on Hayley's finger and kissed her again.

- Isabella would be thrilled if you could let her organise the wedding.

- She would have to get in line because I have two sisters who would probably like to do the same. Wow, I can't believe I am getting married. Again. No white dress for me this time.

- This would be my second wedding too. My first wife ran away from me right after the ceremony. I think I have never told you that.

- Well, you haven't, but Isabella has.

- Great. What else has she told you?

- It doesn't matter, I don't even remember now. Let's go home and celebrate! I think my senses are fine and I can go back to the city.

- Are you sure? It's going to be loud.

- I don't care. I'm so happy that I don't think there is anything that could ruin my day now.

- I heard good news. Congratulations! I am so happy for you two!

Isabella called the minute Hayley walked inside her house. She must have known about the engagement before it actually happened.

- Thanks, Isabella. I really didn't see that coming.

- So, can we start planning your wedding now? I have never done it before and I always wanted to.

- First of all, I need to talk to my sisters. And second of all, I need to disappear now for a few weeks. I am having a surgery and all, remember?

- Oh right! I have forgotten all about it. So where are you two going?

- I think we'll take the boat from Amanda and Tom. Apparently they do not plan on sailing anywhere for a while so we can borrow their yacht.

- Sounds like a good plan. Would you like me to take care of Lexi?

- That would be great! But if you are busy I can ask my sisters.

- No problem at all, you know how much I love this dog.

- Great. Thank you Isabella.

- So, do you have any particular destination in mind?

- Well, I thought we could sail to Hawaii.

- Sounds like a good plan. I hope you two would have a wonderful time. I will pick Lexi up tomorrow morning.

- Thanks again Isabella and see you tomorrow.

Hayley sat on the floor with Lexi's head on her lap. She wanted to spend some quality time with the dog, knowing that she wouldn't see her for the next few weeks.

- I can't believe this is all real, Lexi. I am going to sail with Liam but I will tell my sisters I am going to the clinic in California. I am perfectly healthy although only two days ago I was lying in bed, wondering if I could ever walk again. It all sounds so unreal. If someone had told me this would be my life, I would've never believed them. But here I am, forever young, forever healthy… And I'm engaged. Last year I was so sure I was going to grow old and die alone, unloved and unwanted and now I am getting married. I'm happy, Lexi, I really am. Although I'm scared of what is ahead. But with Liam by my side everything will be OK, right? It has to be. I just need to be strong and don't give up, whatever fate throws at me… But now it's time to focus on my role. I need to convince my sisters that I am truly unwell. I don't want to do it but there is no other way. I can't just tell them the truth, they would freak out… I won't be around for a while, Lexi and your aunty will take you but I will be back, I promise. So don't forget me, OK? And be good.

Hayley leaned and kissed Lexi's head.

- I already miss you, my four-legged friend.

The next day at eight-thirty in the morning Hayley was all packed and ready to go. She was sitting in her wheelchair, waiting for her sisters to arrive. She was so nervous, afraid that something might give her away. And she felt terrible, sitting in that wheelchair, knowing that she didn't belong there. She was so ashamed, thinking about all disabled people and what they would think of her now. She was nailed to bed for only a few days and it felt like hell so she couldn't even imagine what it was like for those who were forced to spend the rest of their life that way. She was so grateful for meeting Liam and getting to be a part of the magical side of the world. It literally saved her life. But now all she could think of was how much she wanted to already be on that boat.

- Good luck – whispered Liam seeing the approaching car. Hayley took a deep breath trying to remain calm.

- Hi sister. How are you feeling?

The sadness and pity written on their faces filled Hayley's eyes with tears. She felt like a fraud and she couldn't even look them in the eye without shame.

- Hi guys. – although she smiled, her voice was breaking, giving away her true emotions - I'm OK, thank you. I have a good feeling about that clinic. Apparently, they have some top-class surgeons over there and they are willing to see me so...

- That's the spirit! - April nearly yelled. - We're so glad to see you so optimistic, Hayley. Seeing you in that hospital was breaking my heart. You always had that cheerful disposition so hold on to it and don't ever lose it.

- I won't. Thank you guys, it means a lot to me that you care so much about me. I love you.

- We love you too. Work hard and do your best and stay save and call us whenever you want, day or night.

- I will… I'll see you soon.

Hayley wanted to wipe the tears from her face before she realised she should not move. She just sniffed then and let the tears leave a few wet spots on her clothes.

- Have a nice journey and please text me when you're there.

- I will. Bye girls.

- Bye.

Liam carried Hayley to the car and put her wheelchair into the trunk. Isabella was already sitting in the back seat as she was supposed to take the car back once they have reached the airport.

- How are you feeling? - She asked when the car started driving, leaving the twins waving on the driveway.

- I feel bad that I am lying to them. I see they worry so much about me and it's breaking my heart, but I think telling them the truth wouldn't be a good idea. I am still struggling to believe what has really happened to me and what I am now... I don't even know how I would tell them about all this… And what if they didn't accept me? What if they hated me? No, I can't tell them. Ever.

- You worry too much, Hayley. - Liam said. - Let's go on our trip and have some fun. You will be calling them often and saying that everything is fine and you're getting better and that will make them feel better. You don't have to tell them the truth, they don't need to know. But if you ever feel you'd like to be honest with them, we'll find the right way to tell them. But it doesn't have to be now.

- You're right Liam, I think too much. Let me switch off and enjoy this trip.

- So, where is Amanda and Tom waiting for you two with their boat?

- Marina Del Rey. They will pick us up from the LA airport.

- Great. You two are going to have a great time!

- That's what we hope for... I am glad my sisters didn't ask any questions about that surgery. I'm afraid I didn't do enough research to make sure there was really a surgery to help me.

- They are just happy there is hope for you, that's all. They don't need to know all the details.

- And what do you plan on doing, Isabella? Now that you can't work because of Lexi.

- I'll just stay home, play with your dog, read a book, go to the cinema. I just want to chill, you know? I don't remember the last time I was home for longer than a few days. It feels like I'm constantly on the road, chasing bad guys. I don't have a solid plan but I'm sure I won't be bored. So take your time and have fun and don't worry about anything.

- And this is exactly what we're intending to do.

Flight took two hours and was quite pleasant. There were not many people onboard therefore it was nice and quiet. The weather was perfect, with no strong winds so the plane sailed smoothly through the cloudless sky. Amanda and Tom picked up Liam and Hayley from the LAX and drove them to Marina Del Rey. The boat was all theirs for the next two weeks. When Liam was preparing the boat, Hayley called her sisters, trying to sound as optimistic as possible.

- Hi girls. The flight was OK and we are now at the clinic. I will have a conversation with my doctor in thirty minutes. Everything is OK.

- Do you have your own room or is there anyone else with you?

- Just me.

- Good. You won't have to worry about anyone snoring. Does it look OK?

- Yes, it's very specious, painted in bright colours. We also have some fresh flowers in the vase.

Hayley couldn't believe how easy it was to lie to her sisters. She didn't even stutter.

- That sounds lovely. Call us when you find out anything.

- I will. Bye.

- Bye.

Hayley was sitting quietly below the deck, staring at the wall, completely disconnected.

- What's the matter?

Liam made her jump. She didn't even notice when he entered the room.

- I just... I realised that the things I'm telling them could be true. I could be at that clinic right now, discussing my surgery.

- Do you regret the decision you made?

- No, I don't regret anything, Liam. I am happy here, with you, ready to sail away. - she kissed him and cuddled up to him. - There's no place I'd rather be. So, what's the plan, captain?

- We are going to Hawaii. Amanda and Tom would pick up their boat there, unless you want to go someplace else?

- How long would it take to get to Hawaii?

- About two weeks. Depends on the weather.

- Is there anything closer? I may get bored here.

- Bored? We have plenty of games and incredibly huge collection of DVDs. I also saw a book or two. We have a satellite connection so you can call your sisters or Isabella whenever you want to.

- I didn't know that, I thought it's just a boat and that's it.

- Don't be silly, Amanda and Tom sail for weeks or even months sometimes, so they need some entertainment too.

- I didn't think about that. I thought they just enjoy the sun and swim with the dolphins... OK then. Hawaii it is.

They spent that evening on playing games on Play Station. It turned out that Hayley was not that bad and made a good rival. Although, she didn't win a single football game, she was pretty good at racing.

- I'm done with games for tonight. – Liam sounded bored - How about a movie?

- Looks like someone doesn't like losing.

Hayley was pleased there was something she was as good at as Liam.

- It's not that, I had fun. I just don't feel like playing anymore. We can always come back to this tomorrow.

- Fair enough. So, what would you like to watch?

They searched through the mountain of DVDs, trying to pick something interesting.

- Lord of The Rings! - Hayley shouted - I haven't seen this one in ages! We need to watch it.

- I didn't know you loved it that much.

- Are you kidding me? It's like the best movie ever! I love everything about it and it's still my number one.

- I think it's OK. There are a few things that I would do differently but in general, yes I admit it is a good movie.

- So what is it that you don't like about the movie?

- I think some scenes are too long or really not needed at all. Especially the ones involving Frodo and Sam.

- But without those scenes the movie would be just one battlefield.

- And would it be so terrible? Also, Gollum's voice is quite annoying.

- Do you want to watch something else?

- No, let's see this one. With you by my side I will definitely enjoy it.

The next four hours they spent in front of a TV, watching the movie and commenting on the scenery, costumes and music. It was nearly two in the morning and Hayley was ready to go to bed when Liam asked her to join him on the deck. He didn't even have to explain what he wanted to show her, she noticed that straight away. She has never seen the sky so full of stars. It was breathtaking.

- I can't believe it's real. I didn't even know there were so many stars. It looks beautiful!

- Have you never watched shooting stars before?

- I have, but it was never that dark outside. There was always a lamp somewhere nearby. Can you see any constellations?

- I can see Pegasus right above us. Can you see that nearly square box made of four stars?

Hayley searched the sky above them, trying to find the constellation but it was too difficult.

- Forget it, there are too many stars and I see no square. But I believe you it's there. So do you know much about astronomy?

- I wouldn't say much, but I know something. When you live forever, you have plenty of time to learn.

- What else do you know apart from star constellations?

- I speak French, Italian and Spanish.

- Impressive.

- I ride horses, play the guitar and piano.

- Violin?

- No, that was too much for me.

- Do you learn faster? Does it come with all the other perks?

- No, I had to spend a lot of time on each of these things, so don't expect you would know everything just by looking at the book. It doesn't work that way.

- Once, I was told I could learn in my sleep, with the textbook under my pillow.

- Did it work?

- No and I failed my test.

- How old were you?

- Seven.

They spent the rest of the night on the deck, watching shooting stars and telling funny stories of their childhood. At dawn, they discovered that the sunrise was as impressive as the sunset and the night sky they have seen earlier. The sky gradually changed from black and navy to purple and red, eventually becoming orange and yellow..

And all these colours reflected nicely on the surface of the water, where the moon and starry sky was showing before.

Shortly after ten, Hayley decided to call her sisters. Every time she reached for her cell phone, her heart started beating faster. She was afraid what questions her sisters might ask. '*What if they ask about the details of the surgery? What if they hear something in the background? Those bloody seagulls are so loud! What if they had done some research on their own and now they know there is no surgery?* She started breathing faster and her hands started to sweat.

- Hi, how are you? What did the doctor say?

- Well, I already had my surgery this morning. I didn't tell you because I didn't want you to worry.

- Oh my god! How did it go? How are you feeling?

- It went well. I can't even tell you exactly what they have done, it's hard to repeat all that complicated medical terminology – Hayley hoped that would be enough to avoid any complicated questions she couldn't possibly answer - But I can feel my feet and my hands so whatever they have done, worked.

- That's great news! We are so happy for you. So what's next?

- Physiotherapy. I may be here for another month or so. There is a lot of hard work ahead of me.

- You can do this, we believe in you. The hardest part is behind you now so from this point, it will only get better.

- I have to go now. I will call you in a couple of days. Don't worry about me, everything is fine.

Hayley hung up and sighted heavily.

- So how much do you know exactly about that fake surgery that you had this morning? - Liam asked.

- That's the thing, I don't know much. I know there is something that can help paralysed patients but I didn't read much about it. There is some nerve transfer or something like that. I don't even know if it's something that could actually help someone like me. I just hoped my sisters wouldn't ask too many questions and thankfully, I was right. They don't want to know all the details so I don't have to explain everything.

- They believe you, that's all that matters.

- Right… I just feel so bad lying to them. It makes me nervous and all those lies make them anxious too.

- I know it's difficult but it's just for now, a few more lies and it's all over, you're back home and life is back to normal.

- Not exactly… I need to be careful so the twins don't come across all that blood I keep in my fridge. And that I don't do any sudden moves or that I don't get too angry and change into a monster. What if I cut myself or hurt myself any other way and they'll see I'm fine?

- Like you said, you just need to be careful. Don't worry Hayley, it will be fine. Don't be too stressed in their company and don't behave like you're made of glass. Just be yourself.

- Who knew that one day it would be the most difficult thing to do, to be myself.

- Life is full of surprises. Now let's go, we're wasting perfectly good weather.

Hayley loved their time on that boat. They swam and played games and watched the stars. Occasionally, Liam wrote a few pages of his new book and Hayley spent that time on talking to Isabella. The weather was great and the ocean was quiet so they reached the cost of Oahu Island within fifteen days as planned. They left the boat in Honolulu Harbor for Amanda and Tom to pick up, found a hotel walking distance from the beach and reserved their room for a few nights. It was very elegant and specious, with an ocean view.

- I could live here, with this view. – said Hayley throwing herself across the bed.

- Why won't you? Nothing stops you from moving here.

- Maybe in a few years, when I have to leave because of my age. I don't feel quite ready yet to leave now… And when I'm sick and tired of the sun and the ocean, we can move to Switzerland and enjoy the Alps.

- Sounds like a good plan. And what do you want to do now?

- I want to eat something. Could you please reserve a table for us?

Liam went downstairs to reserve the table and Hayley took a quick shower and put on one of her black elegant dresses that Liam liked so much.

- You look ravishing, Hayley. Looks like I can't join you in my Hawaiian t-shirt and shorts. Wait for me at the table and order some wine. I will quickly change into something more suitable. Otherwise we'd look like Lady and the Tramp.

Liam joined Hayley a few minutes later, wearing his black suit and a white shirt. They ordered Hawaiian pizza just to check if it tasted any better than in Aspen but they couldn't tell the difference. After dinner, they felt like dancing but the closest bar with the dance floor was playing rock and roll, country and pop so they would look ridiculous there in their smart clothes. They decided to quickly change into something more casual and go dancing. The place was not too crowded and everyone was having a good time. The music seemed too loud at first, but they got used to it eventually. The place smelled of food, beer and sweat but it didn't destroy the nice atmosphere. Everywhere around lied Leis - the popular Hawaiian necklaces made of flowers that everyone got after landing but obviously didn't plan on taking back home as a souvenir.

At eight, the karaoke session started and Liam put his name on the list without hesitation.

- I love karaoke. How about you, Hayley? Will you sing?

- No, this is not for me. I am not a good singer. I prefer singing when nobody listens.

- Come on, you can't be that bad. Go and have some fun.

- I am having fun. I just prefer listening to other people singing.

- Coward.

- Don't say that!

- Then go and sing, I dare you.

Hayley thought for a moment and had a look around the bar. It looked like at least a half of the crowd was already quite drunk. Nobody knew her and nobody would remember her despite how bad she could be.

- Fine, challenge accepted. Go and put my name on the list.

- Great! What will you sing?

- I Feel Like a Woman by Shania Twain.

- Excellent.

They waited patiently for their turn. Some people were pretty good but some sounded like a wounded cat which was exactly how Hayley imagined herself. Liam was first to go. He sang You Can Leave Your Hat On which caught attention of every woman in the restaurant. They were whistling, screaming and clapping. Liam looked very charming and the crowd loved him. When he was leaving the stage, the crowd looked disappointed and wanted him to get back up there and sing again.

- Stop smiling like an idiot, you were not that good.

- Come on, Hayley, looks like everyone else thinks differently. I was great and you just don't want to admit it. Now go on, it's your turn.

Hayley got up and approached the microphone with her legs and hands shaking. She was very nervous, it was her first time singing in front of anyone else than her dog.

- Hi everyone. My name is Hayley and I will be singing Shania Twain's song.

- Yeah, go girl!

The crowd looked very excited. Liam raised the bar quite high and it was going to be hard to impress those people after his excellent performance. The music started playing. Hayley closed her eyes and imagined herself in her living room, singing and dancing around like she has so many times before. She smiled and started singing with her eyes still closed. But when she heard how everyone started clapping and whistling, she opened her eyes and saw everyone smiling, cheering and clearly having a good time. She felt more confident and got carried away by that moment. When she finished, she was happy and very pleased with her little performance.

- I must say you sound pretty good. I don't know why you were so afraid to do it.

- It was great! I had so much fun! I wished I had done it sooner.

- I told you it's fun. You need to be more confident Hayley, you were great up there.

- Thanks Liam. It looks like all these hours spent on singing while driving or cleaning were a good practice. You see… your opinion doesn't matter that much because I know you would tell me anything just to make me feel better but seeing all those strangers enjoying my singing made me believe that I must be quite good indeed.

They stayed in that bar till midnight, listening to others singing. There was no time for them to sing again but they decided to come back the next day. When they left the bar, despite late hour, the streets were just as busy as during the day. Many drunk but happy people walking around, dancing and singing. The night was very warm and pleasant and obviously nobody wanted to waste it on sleeping.

- Do you want to go back to the hotel now? - asked Liam as they started walking among the crowd.

- It depends. Do you have something else in mind?

- Maybe I do. Come with me.

Liam took Hayley by the hand and they went quickly towards the ocean. After a few minutes, they stopped on the edge of a cliff.

- Go on and jump. - Liam said encouragingly.

- Are you nuts? It's too high!

- It is but it won't kill you. I think you will really enjoy the feeling of falling so I think you should give it a go.

- Will it hurt?

- Maybe just a bit and just for a moment but it's still worth it. Would you like me to jump first or do you want me to jump with you?

- Jump first.

- Will you jump too or will I have to come back here for you?

- I will jump, I promise.

Without hesitation, Liam jumped with a loud 'woo hoo' before he hit the water. Three seconds later, Hayley saw him on the surface.

- Come on Hayley! Your turn!

Hayley hesitated. *'I can't die… Liam just did it and he's fine. If he says it's fun I bet it really is. I can't hurt myself so there is nothing to be afraid of. If I don't like it I just won't do it ever again but I need to try once. I have the whole eternity and I can't be afraid to try new things, to take risk. OK… Let's do this.' She* took a deep breath, closed her eyes and jumped. She was falling for a few seconds before she hit the water. It didn't hurt at all and she quickly found her way up to the surface.

- Wow!

She wiped the water from her face.

- You want to do it again?

And so they jumped again and swam a bit in the ocean. Although it was late at night, the water was still warm and pleasant. The sky was cloudless and the full moon lit up the night. One hour later, they were back in their hotel room, completely soaked but happy.

Days were passing by on swimming in the ocean, riding jet skis and dancing on the beach at night. Karaoke was their daily ritual and it was always fun. Liam offered to teach Hayley how to surf but it was not easy so she gave up after an hour. There were plenty of other things to do and she didn't want to waste her time on something that she didn't quite enjoy. Hayley has never felt so free. Even though her future still looked a bit scary and the idea of eternity seemed a bit overwhelming, she has never felt as stress-free and care-free as she did there on that small island, enjoying every moment. Every time Liam was surfing, she was sitting on the beach enjoying the sun. After her transition, her body was never to change again. She would never gain or lose weight, her hair would never grow longer and she would never get tanned. That's why she didn't have to worry about explaining her tan to her sisters. She was supposed to spend all her days on physiotherapy and there was no time for lying on the beach. She called June and April every few days to tell them how much progress she has made and how much better she felt day by day.

After two weeks on that beautiful island, they packed their bags and looked at the ocean one last time. It was a seven-hour flight from Honolulu to Houston and another two-hour flight to Aspen and even an idea of such a long journey made them feel tired. Isabella picked them up and drove them straight to see April and June. Hayley promised her sisters she would pop in so they could see for themselves how she was. Once they have got there, Liam helped Hayley to get out of the car. April and June watched Hayley slowly approaching them on crutches with Liam and Isabella right behind her, making sure she didn't fall.

- Oh my god, look at you Hayley, you're walking! That's so amazing! I am so happy! - April had tears in her eyes.

They hugged Hayley gently as if she was made of a thin glass. They helped her get inside and asked dozens of questions about the surgery, physiotherapy and the clinic. Back in Hawaii, Hayley assumed her sisters could have some questions so she prepared a few answers. Every night before falling asleep, she repeated the description of the clinic she saw online and one of their rooms. She also had a look at the exercises advised after a back surgery and she carefully learnt them by heart so now she could describe her time in California without stuttering. Once the twins have noticed Hayley was doing OK, they started talking about themselves so Hayley breathed a sigh of relief that her part was over. After one hour, she said she was tired after the flights and she wanted to get some rest. The twins walked her back to the car and waved her goodbye. Hayley knew she would not see them any time soon. They didn't have to worry about her anymore so there was no reason to keep calling or visiting. Their relationship was back to normal meaning that an occasional phone call was all she could expect from now on.

Chapter 11

Hayley was trying to get back to her old life. She saw a few of her regular clients and devoted her free time to Lexi. By now, she got used to her new heightened senses and the need to drink blood. But it was her first week alone since she turned. Liam needed to fly to New York as his next book was about to be released and his presence was requested. Even though he called daily and was happy to keep Hayley a company at night, she wanted to learn to manage on her own. She didn't want to create an impression that she was addicted to him and needed him constantly by her side.

A few nights in a row, she was losing sleep. It was difficult to fall asleep without feeling tired and sleepy. During her trip with Liam, she barely slept but there was always something to do, however at home, all those sleepless nights just made her think. It has been over a year now since she was attacked that cold October night. And it was the first time that year she thought about her husband. She thought about how he died – a car accident caused by someone's reckless driving. Three teenagers who had too much fun driving a fast car they have stolen from a daddy. They were not only stupid but also very drunk and the only reason those boys were not in prison was because they were minors. Hayley was wondering what their lives have looked like for the past two years. Whether they regretted what they've done and were haunted by the recurring nightmares or whether they quickly forgot about the accident and happily lived their lives as if nothing has happened. Even though she was heartbroken, full of anger and indescribably suffering, she couldn't do anything about it back then because there was nothing she could have done, but now, with her strength, she could avenge her husband and bring him justice.

- I could pay them a little visit – she said to Lexi, cuddling up to her in a perfectly dark bedroom where even the soft light of the new moon did not reach through the blinds – I could make them scared, make them regret…

She decided not to mention anything to Liam as she didn't want him to be a part of it. It was her problem and she needed to deal with it on her own. She looked at her cell phone, it was three in the morning. She sighed loudly with annoyance having realised she needed some help after all, she needed Isabella to use her connections to get the names and addresses of those three boys. Hayley couldn't possibly find them herself. She thought intensively for a few minutes before she reached for her phone again. She was sure Isabella was not asleep and she knew she would ask questions without blindly revealing all the information, not knowing what it was for.

- Hayley, I can help you get that information, it will be easy, but I need to know first what you plan on doing once I have given it to you.

Isabella was not stupid, she knew Hayley wanted a revenge but there were many ways to punish someone and she hoped these boys wouldn't pay for their stupidity with their lives.

- I just want to see how they are. Maybe I could scare them a bit, just like you scare your bounties. I need to do something Isabella, I can't just make my peace with it. There was no punishment for what they've done and now I am able to make them finally pay.

- Just promise me you won't do anything stupid.

- I promise. I won't kill them if that's what you think, you know me, you know I couldn't possibly do that.

- OK, I will ask around about these boys.

- Thank you and could you please keep it from Liam? This is about my ex-husband and I don't feel comfortable talking about it with him, he doesn't need to know.

- Of course, I won't say a word.

Hayley didn't have to wait too long for Isabella to get all the information. By the end of the next day, she knew the names and addresses and even where they went to school. She had their photos too. She spent her sleepless nights on thinking what she would do to them. She wanted them terrified, crying, begging for mercy, just like Mr Brown when he met Isabella. She wanted them to spend the rest of their lives afraid of their own shadows and then and only then, Hayley could move on with her life.

It was a cold November evening, unusually bright as the snow was reflecting the light of a full moon and the sky was cloudless. The boys had a small bonfire right outside the city, in a company of three young girls who looked too young to drink. They were all having fun, drinking and laughing and Hayley hated it. She watched them for a few minutes thinking what to do about the girls, there was no need to scare them, they did nothing wrong and didn't deserve a trauma. Hayley was walking back and forth behind the tense line of trees and bushes. '*Maybe I should go home and try some other day.* – she thought – *maybe this is a sign that I should let go or think it through again. Maybe it is a sign that I should change my mind and walk away when I still have a chance…*' But she couldn't walk away, their laughter made her angry, they didn't deserve to be happy and have fun. She could feel the growing anger making her heart beat faster and her hands shake. She emerged from behind the trees and approached the group with her fists clenched. They all looked at her with surprise as they were sure there was nobody around and

they were all alone. There was no footpath nearby and
nobody knew about that place apart from a few teenagers.

- Hey, lady, are you lost?

But Hayley didn't answer.

- What's wrong with her?

- I think she's crazy or something.

Boys started laughing but the girls were a bit scared.
Hayley looked at them, her eyes turned black, her self-
control was fading away and her emotions were taking
over.

- You three, get out of here, now.

The girls quickly disappeared behind the trees, leaving
their bags by the fire. They didn't even turn around. They
couldn't see Hayley's face as she was standing too far
away from the fire but her posture and tone of voice made
them aware that the situation was serious and there was no
reason to stick around and see what's going to happen
next.

- Hey, what the hell is your problem? Are you looking
for trouble?

Hayley looked at the boys.

- Bradley Evans. Does it ring a bell?

The boys got all serious now, it was clear they
remembered that name.

- He's dead because of you. – Hayley continued - My
husband is dead because of you!

The boys looked at one another, feeling nervous and
ashamed.

- Listen, ma'am, it was an accident, alright? We didn't
mean to hurt anyone. – They didn't mean to be
disrespectful anymore, the situation was no longer funny.

- I don't care what you think. You killed a good man
and you never paid for it. But you will pay now.

Hayley got to the first boy within the blink of an eye
and hit his face hard with her fist. The boy fell, his nose
was heavily bleeding and Hayley's punch literally crushed

his face, leaving him unrecognisable. When he started chocking on his blood, the other two boys started to run. Hayley pushed one of them aside. The boy flew a few meters across the field and hit his head on the tree, leaving a bloody mark on the bark. She quickly got to the last one, the talkative one, the one she blamed the most although she didn't know for sure he was the one driving that night.

- No... please... I'm sorry!

Hayley was holding him up against the tree with his feet above the ground. He quickly realised how strong she was and that he couldn't stand a chance with her. He started to cry, struggling to catch his breath with Hayley's fingers around his neck. She didn't even know how strong her grip was until she heard the sound of breaking bones. The boy died instantly, not saying anything else. Hayley let him fall on the ground, caught a deep breath and looked around. One boy was lying on the ground by the fire, covered in blood, his eyes wide open. The other one was by the tree a few meters away, completely still. The third one was at Hayley's feet, with his neck crushed. None of them was alive. With her vampire hearing she could hear no other heartbeat but hers. There was nobody around, the boys were dead.

- Oh my god... What have I done?

Hayley panicked. She had a look around and covered her mouth with disbelieve, spreading boys' blood all over her cheeks. She looked at her hands, covered in blood, not shaking but perfectly still, like steady hands of a good surgeon. Although she was terrified of what she's done, her body was perfectly calm.

- No, no, no... It can't be real. This is not happening.

In that moment, her eyes filled with tears and she couldn't catch her breath. The world around her swirled and she passed out.

Chapter 12

Hayley woke up in a room that she didn't recognise. There was a drip connected to her arm and some beeping monitors by the bed. She was confused and unsure how she got into a hospital. She tried to lift herself up leaning on her hands but her arms shook making her aware how dizzy and weak she was. *'Why am I feeling this way? I'm a vampire, I should be fine'* She eventually managed to sit on the edge of her bed. She felt stiff and numb as if she was lying for days.

- Hayley! You're awake, thank god. Don't get up.

April helped Hayley get back to bed.

- April, what are you doing here?

She asked although it was the least important question on her list. *'Who brought me here? Are the police outside? Am I going to prison? Why am I feeling so weak? What's happened to me? Does Liam know what I've done?'* Hayley's head began to ache under the stream of thought.

- Nurse called me – answered April - You put me and June as your next of kin after Bradley died.

- Why am I here?

April sat on the edge of the bed. She looked concerned and tired, with her eyes red and watery. She gently stroked Hayley's hand.

- What's the last thing you remember?

Hayley couldn't say she remembered being in the woods, surrounded by three dead bodies. Maybe her sister didn't know all the details and she shouldn't risk giving too much information.

- I am not sure. Do you know what happened?

- I think you should talk to the doctor, he can answer all your questions.

April got up and called the doctor who came right away. It was not the same man who treated her after the car accident. It was an older man, tall and skinny, clearly having years of experience in medicine. He wore big round glasses covering most of his wrinkled face, his short beard was all grey and he was bald.

- Good morning Mrs Evans. I'm glad to see you alive. How are you feeling?

'Evans? I'm Anderson now, I updated all my records.' – she thought but decided not to pick on that, there were more important things to discuss.

- Dizzy, a bit sick and very confused… Why am I here, doctor?

- One of your clients, miss Henderson, called us when she saw you through the window. You were lying on your sofa and didn't respond to the doorbell. She was afraid you were dead and you nearly were, Mrs Evans. We performed gastrointestinal lavage to get rid of benzodiazepines.

Hayley was getting more and more confused with every word. She didn't remember taking any pills.

- Now, Mrs Evans, we don't know whether you simply took too much by mistake and it was just an accident or whether you were trying to take your own life.

- What?! Why would I do that? Why would I want to kill myself?!

- We know your husband died last year and we are afraid you are still grieving and struggling with your loss. I can let you go as there is nothing threatening your life anymore, Mrs Evans, but I would like you to be examined by our psychologist first. Is that OK?

Hayley didn't answer. She didn't even move. She was staring at the doctor, trying to understand what was going on. Nothing made sense. One minute she was a vampire, ruthlessly killing three teenagers and the next minute she's human again, in a hospital after a suicide attempt. Her husband died over two years ago and she was doing fine, living her new life the best she could, surrounded by family and friends.

- Doctor, I did not try to kill myself, I am not suicidal. I will talk to your psychologist so my sister can take me home.

- I'm happy to hear that. You can change into your clothes now and I will let Dr Carter know that you'll come over soon. Take care of yourself Mrs Evans.

Hayley looked at April. Her face was very serious and tense.

- I'm fine April, don't worry.

- Be honest with me, did you try to kill yourself, Hayley?

- No, I did not. Why would I want to kill myself April? I'm fine. It's a misunderstanding, that's all, so stop worrying.

She managed to smile, hoping it would convince April but her sister was still looking at her suspiciously.

- Did you talk to Liam?

- Who's Liam?

Hayley was trying to put all the pieces together. How much of what she remembered was actually real? And how much of what actually happened didn't she remember?

- Never mind.

Dr Carter was a lady in her sixties, short and chubby with large, thick, round glasses with a silver chain and grey hair neatly braided into a long plait. Hayley sat down in a large soft armchair, trying to look relaxed and calm. The doctor quickly read through the medical report and looked at Hayley up and down, analysing her appearance.

- Good morning Hayley. I see you are a psychologist yourself so I am really surprised to see you here. Could you please tell me in your own words what's happened?

- I took too many pills, that's all. I wasn't careful and I learnt my lesson the hard way.

- Why did you take the pills, Hayley?

'I don't know, doctor, I have no foggiest idea why I took those pills. I don't even remember doing it so how should I answer your question?'

- I had a rough day and I felt blue.

- What's happened that day?

- Nothing… I… It was very busy and… at the end of the day I started thinking about my husband and I was sad.

- It's perfectly normal to miss your husband Hayley and to think about him.

- I know. I know how to deal with grief and I am doing fine. Just… Every now and then I feel a bit sad and start reminiscing. I didn't want to feel that way so I took some pills to relax but I am not suicidal, doctor.

- Tell me, what makes you happy?

- Playing with my dog, hiking, skiing, watching sunrises and sunsets, hanging out with my friends… I can keep going on and on with that list, doctor. I know how to enjoy my life.

- So in general, would you say you're happy?

- Yes – Hayley said that with a smile – Yes I am happy.

The smile was genuine and Hayley sounded very convincing. After an hour-long conversation, Dr Carter decided, it's safe to let Hayley go as she didn't seem suicidal. She recommended her to stay away from pills and try herbal medicine instead. She advised going someplace nice and trying to relax. She gave Hayley her card and asked her to get in touch in case she felt depressed or had any sleeping problems.

April drove Hayley home, not saying anything in the car. But the silence didn't bother Hayley, she had far too much on her plate to worry about April being angry with her. She would take care of it later, but now, she needed to remember what's happened.

- Hayley, would you like something to eat? – asked April as they parked at Hayley's driveway.

- No, I'm not hungry. Go home April, I see you're tired. And don't worry about me. I'm fine. I promise.

- OK. But if you need anything, just call, OK? Any time, day or night. Me and June are here for you and we love you and we care for you. I hope you know that.

- I know and I love you too. I'm sorry I put you through all of this. No more pills, you have my word.

- I'm glad you're OK. Talk to you later?

- Sure. Bye April.

Hayley waved April goodbye and went inside her house. Everything looked normal.

- Lexi!

Hayley called her dog but Lexi didn't come. She went to the kitchen and realised there were no bowls in the corner. There was no leash on the wall and no toys on the floor. Everything was gone as if Lexi never existed. *'She's probably with the twins –* she thought *– but what if… what if she's not? Maybe something else happened that I don't remember? April reacted so weird when I asked about Liam.'* Hayley grabbed her laptop and quickly logged into her bank account. She went through her statements, carefully reading all the transactions from September last year. There was no single transaction from the pet store. Then, she realised she was looking at the wrong year. She was staring at the calendar for a few minutes with disbelieve. Today was twentieth of August last year. *'I don't understand… Did I go back in time? Can witches turn back time? Maybe Isabella found out what I've done and asked Sarah for help? But why would she go back so far? I met them in October which means, technically, we don't know each other yet… I bought Lexi on sixth of September but she was advertised for over a month, which means she should be available now.'*

Hayley found the website she used for her dog search before. She narrowed her search to Colorado Springs but Lexi was not advertised there. She clicked through all adverts but she didn't find her dog.

- I don't understand… Do I have to wait till the sixth of September? Will it all happen again?

She grabbed her cell phone and dialled Liam's number which she knew by heart, it was no longer showing in her contacts.

- Hello?

- Liam? – she asked with her voice higher than usual. Her heart was beating like crazy and her hands were shaking.

- No, it's Henry. Wrong number.

The call disconnected. Hayley stormed out and ran to Liam's house. She pressed the door handle but the door was locked so she knocked. Some young brunette opened.

- Can I help you?

- Hi, I'm looking for Liam.

- I'm sorry, you've got the wrong address. I don't know any Liam.

Hayley turned around and started slowly walking back home. She couldn't understand what was going on. Liam was supposed to live there for a few years now.

She came back home and sat on a sofa with her shoes still on. Nothing made sense and she couldn't find any reasonable explanation. At first, she suspected going back in time but what about the hospital? And the suicide attempt? She had no recollection of that happening last year. *'What's happened to me? Where's Liam? Where's Lexi? What about those boys I've killed?* She was scared, clueless and helpless. She lay down on the sofa, hugging her knees with her arms like a scared child. She pressed her wet with tears face against a pillow and quickly fell asleep.

Hayley woke up a few hours later feeling cold. The sun was long gone, the window was open and she was not covered with any blankets. She got up, put on a hoodie and had a look around the living room. It looked so empty and quiet and that view made her cry again. She sat on the sofa and hid her face in her hands, resting her elbows on her knees.

– I have no idea what to do - she said aloud even though there was nobody there – What should I do now? How should I live? I wish there was some explanation, I wish it was not happening.

She took a deep breath trying to calm down. When she went to the kitchen and opened her fridge she realised it was nearly empty. No milk, no bread, only some unopened package of cheese and some eggs. She called the near-by restaurant and ordered a proper dinner. She didn't feel like going shopping or cooking, she couldn't focus on anything with her head full of questions. She went upstairs to take a quick shower as she had at least half an hour before her food was going to be delivered. She was out right in time to open the door for the delivery man. She took the food, sat in the kitchen and started eating straight from the box, not bothering to reach for a plate. She was staring at the table surface, deep in thought, looking numb and pensive. Having eaten, she went back to the sofa, covered herself with a blanket and fell asleep.

The next day, Hayley stayed in bed for another thirty minutes thinking what to do. She knew she needed to make a solid decision and force herself to do something meaningful, otherwise, she would end up sleeping all days and crying all nights. She needed to use her knowledge of psychology and help herself as she has helped her patients. Even though she felt like going back to sleep, she got up, got dressed and went shopping. She spent the whole day going from one chore to another, making sure the fridge was full, the dinner was ready and the house was clean. In the evening, she decided she would go back to seeing her clients and living her life the way she did before she met Liam. She also decided to wait till the sixth of September and try to get Lexi, though the chances were small the dog would be again available. With Liam not living in his old house, the time travel seemed even more impossible. But the only explanation Hayley had was that Sarah used her magic to turn back time so she could make all right decisions. But apart from killing those three boys, Hayley didn't regret anything. She was glad she met Liam and she would turn into a vampire once again so they could be together. She liked her life with him and she truly loved him. She decided she would get Lexi and then go out that cold October night so she could be attacked again and saved by Liam again. She was not going to change anything. If only she was given that chance.

Days were passing by fast as Hayley kept herself busy. She had as many patients in one day as possible, having no time for herself. She talked to her sisters every day and it brought them closer. Their bond was getting stronger day by day and Hayley was surprised how easy it was to talk to the twins, laugh with them or ask for advice. They used to be close when she was taking care of them after their parents died but then, the gap grew bigger. Hayley became a grown up with her serious problems and responsibilities and the twins were still unreasonable, silly and thinking about having fun. As they had each other, Hayley decided to let them be, being sure they would turn to her if in any trouble. But now, they became her friends and she liked having them around, listening to their crazy stories. They easily took Hayley's mind off her current problems and even made her laugh. But it hurt her that she couldn't be as honest with her sisters as they were with her and that she couldn't tell them everything that was truly bothering her.

On the fifth of September, Hayley went to the pet store and got all stuff ready for Lexi. She missed her very much and couldn't wait to see her again. The house seemed so empty, cold and quiet without her. She got everything like last time, making sure her favourite toys and food were ready. She couldn't wait to see her happy dog face, with her ears turned back and her tail wagging as if it was about to fall off.

On the sixth of September, after an intensive day in work, Hayley made herself a cup of green tea and sat down by the desk in her office. She entered the website and checked all adverts from Colorado Springs but Lexi was not there. At first, she was excited and happy but with every next advertisement, she was getting more and more annoyed.

- I don't understand, she was supposed to be here. Why isn't she here?!

Hayley panicked. It looked as if she was not back in time after all and she couldn't make the same decisions now. She expected that but quietly held on to the hope that maybe she was wrong. She needed to believe that everything would be just the same one day and she just needed to be patient. She got up aggressively and let the chair roll away and hit the wall.

- What the hell happened to me? It was real! I know it was real! It doesn't make any sense!

Hayley started to cry, afraid she was losing her mind. She remembered everything vividly and yet, she was afraid it was all just a dream. She cried for a few hours before she finally fell asleep sitting at her desk, with her face rested on a closed laptop.

Hayley woke up suddenly at the dawn as if someone or something woke her up.

- The diary!

She yelled and ran upstairs to her bedroom. Out of the blue, it came to her that she used to have a diary. She stopped writing in it shortly after she got Lexi. That puppy was taking too much of her attention, then she met Liam and completely forgot about her journal. Hayley aggressively opened the wardrobe and searched through it, scattering her clothes all over the room. She found her diary right in the corner, hidden under a pile of old clothes that she should have gotten rid of a long time ago but always forgot to. She opened her diary on the last page. It was dated eighteenth of August this year.

'This is it. I can't stand it anymore. This sorrow and loneliness are eating me alive. I thought I could get through it like anyone else but I can't. My work is my whole life now and I hate it! But when I don't work I think about Brad and how much I miss him. I can't live this life all by myself. I'm afraid there is no more happiness for me, that there's only pain and loneliness ahead. Everything reminds me of him, I see him in every man I pass by on the street, I can still hear his voice in my head. I can't sleep in my bed when he's not by my side. Nothing brings me joy anymore. Every day feels like a nightmare. I can't sleep, I can't eat… My Dear Sisters, if you ever read this, I'm sorry. I love you.'

- Oh my god – Hayley sat on the bed, dropping her diary on the floor - So I did try to kill myself after all… But why don't I remember any of this? Side effects of the pills I've taken? Is my mind playing tricks on me?

Hayley slowly started to realise that all she remembered was a dream. Lexi, Liam, her accident, turning into a vampire… it all was in her head, when she was lying in that hospital, fighting for her life. Maybe, subconsciously, she wanted to convince herself there was still a chance for a better life? That there was still hope and reasons to live? That she may love again? Hayley put her diary back to the wardrobe and slowly tidied up the room. *'I can understand why I imagined Liam as a vampire, I wanted a saviour, a strong, invincible man who would not be taken away from me like Brad was. I wanted an immortal man who would always be by my side, that makes sense... But why did I dream about the accident? Why did I imagine something so terrible? To show myself how bad life can be? To make myself understand that I can get through my grief and live because I'm young and healthy?* Hayley came back to her office and sat back in her chair. She turned the computer on and entered a website of a local dog shelter.

- OK, let's get a dog. At least that much I can do, at least this one thing can be real.

She couldn't imagine her life without Lexi. That dog brought her so much happiness and turned her world upside down in a good way and she needed her back in her life. Hayley scrolled through the whole website. There were so many dogs looking for home and she felt for all of them. But one dog particularly caught her eye. It was a beautiful eight-month-old black German Shepherd. She was already fully grown, completely black, with pointy ears and long coat. There was something about her eyes. The sadness and fear Hayley saw in those eyes looked very familiar.

- There's my real Lexi.

Hayley quickly grabbed the wallet and the car keys and drove to the shelter. It was not too far away, only a five-minute drive. When she left the car, she could hear the dogs barking even though she couldn't see any yet. She came inside and approached the front desk There was a young girl in front of a computer screen, with a heavy make-up, pierced lower lip and a name tag saying Vicky.

- Hi, I'd like to adopt one of your dogs. – said Hayley with a gentle smile.

- Hi, I'm really happy to hear that. Are you looking for anything specific or would you like to have a look around?

- Actually, I am interested in your black German Shepherd, if she's still here.

- Let me check... Yes, she's still here. Please, follow me.

Vicky took a leash from the wall and started walking down the corridor.

- Is this your first dog?

- No… I mean yes… Kind of.

Thankfully, Vicky didn't comment on that. They were passing by many cages. Some dogs were barking and jumping around trying to attract Hayley's attention, and some were sitting quietly, probably knowing Hayley was not there for them. They finally got to the right cage. The dog was sitting in the far-right corner, looking exactly as in the photo Hayley saw online. She was terrified and sad, looking at Hayley but not leaving her spot.

- She is a big dog but she's very gentle so don't worry, she won't bite.

Vicky opened the cage and slowly got inside. Hayley followed.

- Come on, girl. Today is your day, you're getting out of here.

They approached the dog. It got up but didn't move forward. Hayley got down to its level and let it sniff her hand. The dog waved its tail a little bit.

- I promise to make your life much better if you promise to do the same for me.

Hayley reached to her pocket and gave the dog some treats. It licked them off of Hayley's hand and waved its tail again. Vicky smiled.

- I think she likes you. You two will get on just fine.

She gave Hayley the leash and left the cage. Hayley looked at the dog.

- Come on girl, let's go home.

Hayley pulled lightly on the leash and the dog started to follow. She filled in all the paperwork and made her donation.

- Thank you Mrs Evans. Do you know what you are going to call her?

- Lexi. Her name is Lexi.

- Sounds great. Well, I hope you two will have a beautiful life together. If there is anything you need from us or you have any questions, give us a call.

- Thanks Vicky.

Hayley started walking towards her car and Lexi was walking right behind. When she opened the door, Lexi got inside immediately, she didn't need any extra encouragement.

- Good girl, there you go.

Hayley gave her a few more treats. She clipped the seatbelt to the collar and started driving home.

- I hope you'll like your new home. I promise to take a good care of you.

When they got home, Hayley opened the door for Lexi and let her have a look around. The dog walked in slowly, with her nose down to the floor. Before Hayley went out, she has left a few treats around the house for Lexi to find. She wanted to give the dog a little encouragement to explore the house and it worked. Lexi was walking from one room to another, finding all treats without any problems. Every now and then, she stopped and had a look around before she started searching for another treat. Hayley sat down on the floor, leaning her back against sofa. She didn't want to stress Lexi by following her around so she got her diary out and started writing.

'I had an extraordinary journey when I was lying in the hospital fighting for my life. I saw what it could look like and I realised I could love again and be happy. My visions were magical and very unbelievable and yet, they felt so real. I know now that there is still so much to live for. Things I have never done and places I have never seen. It makes me sad that the world I have seen in my dreams doesn't exist. I fell in love with Liam and I got used to an idea of being a vampire. I liked my life. I can't make the same decisions but at least now I know what can make me happy. I decided I would start with getting myself a dog.

Lexi from my dreams brought me so much happiness and I believe my new, real Lexi will do the same. Next thing on my list is to go out and meet new people. Give love another chance. I also want to travel, to see Hawaii. And try karaoke. Maybe I can rent a boat and sail a bit myself, swim with the dolphins, watch shooting stars, see the sunrise sitting on the beach. I can find a bit of happiness in all these things. I know it now. It looks like I had to nearly die to understand how to live. I have a second chance now and I will definitely make use of it. My heart tells me that everything is going to be OK.'

Hayley stopped writing and noticed Lexi was sitting on the floor in front of her. She must have found all treats by now.

- You haven't seen the garden yet. Come on, I'll let you out.

Hayley got up, went to the garden and sat on a chair. The dog started walking around the garden with her nose in the grass, focused and excited.

- I knew you would like it here. Let's stay home today. I'll take you for a walk tomorrow. I don't want to overwhelm you, I can only imagine how much information you are getting from all these smells.

It was nice and warm outside. Beautiful golden autumn. Hayley decided to stay in the garden and enjoy the sun. She could never tell when the first snow would fall so she wanted to enjoy every single warm day before onset winter. She was sitting in the sun, relaxing, trying not to think about anything and Lexi was lying in the middle of the garden, chewing on a stick she found in the grass. She was relaxed and much happier than she was that morning. It was a heart-warming view that made Hayley smile.

- Everything is going to be OK – she said looking at Lexi – we have each other now. *I'm no longer alone.*

Lexi woke Hayley up at six next morning. She was sniffing her ear and ticking her with the whiskers. Hayley scratched her ear and gently pushed Lexi away.

- Oh come on, don't tell me you will wake me up at six every day. I am not an early bird. Eight is the earliest you would get me out of bed so get used to it and go away!

Hayley put the blanket over her head and tried to fall asleep again. Lexi realised it was not her time for breakfast yet so she lied down on a rug by the bed and waited patiently for Hayley to get up.

The alarm woke them both up at eight.

- Rule number one – said Hayley as she was preparing food for Lexi - stay quiet till eight. Unless you really need to go out then you can wake me up. But only then.

They both ate their breakfast and went to the garden. The morning sun was not there yet and it was quite chilly in the shade. Hayley came back inside right in time to hear the doorbell. She checked before she opened the door. It was a courier.

- Good morning, Mrs Hayley Evans?
- That's right.
- I have a package for you. Could you please sign here for me?

Hayley signed the papers and took the package. She didn't order anything and wasn't expecting any delivery so the box really piqued her interest. She put the parcel on the kitchen table and carefully opened the box. Inside, there was a book, a very old one, nearly falling apart, brown with yellow pages. There was also a small box with a silver ring with an emerald stone which looked exactly like Leah's ring that Hayley got from Liam in her dreams.

- Oh my god… That's impossible…

Hayley was shocked. Her heart started beating faster and her hands started shaking. In the parcel, there were also two letters, one was sealed and the other one was not so Hayley started reading the second one fist:

'Dear Mrs Evans. Your aunt Eleonora Stone has passed away recently. She has included you in her will, therefore you are now receiving a diary, a sliver ring and a letter in the envelop with a wax seal. Feel free to contact me with any questions.'

The letter was sent from a solicitor.

- Eleonora Stone? I didn't even know her so how did she know me?

Hayley unsealed the letter. It was handwritten and difficult to read.

'My Dearest Hayley, I am your mother's cousin. I live in Alaska and I guess you have never heard about me. The items I am sending you belonged to your ancestor and have been passed through generations. They are our family heirloom so please take a good care of them. I am leaving these for you now as you are the oldest of your generation therefore they are rightfully yours. I hope you'll find them useful. I am sorry we didn't have a chance to meet. I wish you all the best. E.S.'

Hayley took the ring and put it on her finger. It fit perfectly. She looked at it for a minute, gently stroking the emerald stone. It reminded her of Liam and the day he gave it to her. She remembered it vividly as if it had happened yesterday. She sat down with a loud sigh and gently opened the book, making sure not to tear any pages. It was in fact a journal. A very old one, handwritten.

'My mother has just told me she is a witch and I am one too. It scared me. She showed me some simple spells to make me feel better, so I could use my magic instead of being afraid of it. She said my education was about to begin and there is so much I need to learn. I decided to make notes of everything I need to remember. She also advised me to start writing down how I feel, that it would help me accept the magic and understand myself better.'

- I can't believe it… Is this really happening or am I dying again?

Hayley was excited and fascinated but also terrified as she started doubting her sanity. The last time something like that happened, she was dying in a hospital bed so how could she trust it was all real now? She got up and started nervously walking around the kitchen, biting her nail. When she saw Lexi suddenly appearing in the kitchen door, she decided to take a walk to clear her mind and calm down.

- Come on Lexi, time for a walk.

'What is going on? Why did I get all this just now? Who was that Eleonora Stone? Why has my mother never mentioned her to me? Is it all real this time or am I dreaming it all again? Am I a witch? Are April and June witches? Is that ring magical? Are vampires real too? Is Liam real? How come this ring looks exactly like the one from my dreams? Or maybe I just want it to look alike, maybe it's a standard style, after all, there is nothing unusual about it… I bet I could get a ring like that anywhere… And what about that journal? Is it written by a real witch? No…How could it be? That's impossible… I bet I am imagining it again. Maybe I should see someone about it, maybe I should talk to someone professionally… But then, maybe they'd lock me away… No, I should not tell anyone about it. If I'm losing my mind, I should keep it to myself.'

Hayley was walking ahead, pulled by Lexi. She didn't even pay any attention to where they were going. After one hour, Hayley finally started paying attention and realised where they were. They were about a half an hour away from home and fifteen minutes away from the park so she decided she would take Lexi to the park so she could play with other dogs and have some fun. Once they got to the park, Lexi pulled Hayley towards other dogs as she really wanted to play with them. Hayley let her go and sat on the bench watching Lexi running around, barking and playing with other dogs. That view took Hayley's mind off her problems. She was now completely focused to make sure Lexi didn't cause any issues, after all, it was her first time in that park. It was another beautiful sunny day before winter, warm and pleasant so Hayley didn't mind sitting in the park. She took a deep breath and had a look around. The place was full of people. Mothers with their small children, walking slowly, letting them pick up a few colourful leaves lying on the ground. A jogging couple, discussing their plans for the thanksgiving. Dog owners looking into their phones, mindlessly following their dogs. A few men struggling to rake the leaves while the wind relentlessly blew them all over the park. '*It all looks so real*' – thought Hayley – '*god knows if this is a real life or just my mind playing tricks on me again. I guess I'll never know.*' She closed her eyes, tilted her head back and let the autumn sun gently warm her face.

Hayley spent the next two weeks on training Lexi and reading the journal. She didn't see any of her clients as she was miles away deep in thought too many times. She couldn't stop thinking about her dream and how it was connected to the ring and the journal she received so unexpectedly. She read about a young, teenage witch who was gradually discovering her powers. The girl was also describing her day-to-day life in a small village and how difficult it was. It must have been around seventeenth or eighteenth century. It was fascinating and consuming Hayley completely. Every moment that she didn't devote to Lexi, she spent on reading. One day, she came across a proper spell with the instruction of how to perform it. It was one of the easiest spells that the young witch was trying to master. It was supposed to make small objects move without touching.

- Quo volo te moves – Hayley whispered a few times, making sure her pronunciation was correct.

She raised her right hand with her fingers gently bended and her palm raised towards the pen lying on her desk. She took a deep breath and repeated the spell keeping her eyes on the pen. But the item didn't move an inch. It was perfectly still.

- That's just stupid.

She closed the journal with annoyance, turned the light off and went to bed.

It was a cold rainy day, end of September and Hayley was out with Lexi on one of her daily walks. Suddenly, on her path, she noticed a girl who looked remarkably familiar. *'Oh my god, it's Sarah!'* Hayley recognised the witch from her dreams. Without giving it another thought, she approached the girl to talk to her. She was sure Sarah wouldn't recognise her but she needed to check it anyway.

- Hi... could you please tell me what time it is? My phone is dead.

It was an innocent question, it didn't mean anything.

- Hi, sure, it's half past five.

- Thanks a lot.

- No problem Hayley.

The girl started to walk away and Hayley was just standing there, with her jaw down. But she couldn't let her go away, they needed to talk.

- Hey! Wait! How do you know me?

Sarah didn't reply.

- Listen, I really need to talk to you. Could you please come with me?

Sarah hesitated for a second but eventually she agreed to go with Hayley. Her house was literally around the corner, they got inside and took their wet jackets off.

- Would you like some tea?

- Yes, please. It's really cold out there today. I think winter is coming very soon.

Hayley quickly put the kettle on. She didn't even care about Lexi leaving dirty paw prints all over the rug and the floor.

- Tell me all you know about me. – Hayley quickly cut to the chase.

- Well, I don't want to freak you out too much.

- Freak me out? Look at me! I have been freaking out since I woke up in the hospital. I am a complete mess! I don't know what's going on and I think I'm losing my mind so please, tell me what you know.

Hayley sat down completely forgetting about the kettle. Sarah was a bit reluctant but the fear and confusion showing in Hayley's eyes were difficult to ignore.

- OK… I am a witch.

That didn't surprise Hayley and she didn't comment on that so Sarah continued.

- Sometimes the ancestors talk to us and your ancestor contacted me a few weeks ago. She said you were in a hospital, fighting for your life. She created a dream for you to show you that life could be good and there was so much to live for. She just wanted to save your life, Hayley, she wanted to help you.

- She helped me very much. She did save my life. All those things she showed me… But why Liam? Who is he? Is he even real?

- Because he is a good man. Leah knows you two can be happy together. You both need each other.

- So what I saw in my dreams was Leah's vision? Her idea of what my life could look like?

- Exactly.

- What about Fiona? And the accident? Why did she show me that?

- I don't know, I'm sorry.

- What about the ring?

Hayley took the ring off and handed it to Sarah. She was staring at it for a few seconds.

- In my dream, this ring was protecting me from vampires.

- No, it's not that… I think this ring will protect you from getting old… or sick.

- Really?

- But it doesn't make you immortal so be careful, you still can get hurt.

Hayley put the ring back on her finger.

- So you're saying that I will never go to a doctor again and I won't age as long as I wear it?

- Correct. It's a very powerful item.

Hayley stared at the ring for a minute, not saying anything, trying to put together all pieces of information Sarah has just told her.

- Thank Leah for it when you talk to her next… If you talk to her ever again… So what am I supposed to do now? Where can I find Liam? Did Leah give you any instructions for me?

- She didn't say anything else. I'm sorry but I don't have all the answers.

- That's OK, you already helped me a lot. You shed some light on a few things… Do you know why I'm not a witch?

- Not everyone in the family is. The magic is passed through generations but not to everyone.

- Right… So it's possible that one of my sisters can be a witch…

- Yes, that's possible. But I guess if nothing magical happened so far, they are not witches. There is a small chance though that their magic remains dormant.

- So Leah knew I was dying and that's why she created that dream? Sorry, I just want to make sure I understand what's happened.

- Yes, that's exactly what's happened. She knew you wouldn't die so she wanted to give you a reason to live. I don't know anything about Liam and I may ask her when I have a chance but I'm guessing there is a reason why she didn't give away all the information. She's done her part by showing you a nice image of your new life and she let you meet the love of your life. Now is your turn to put some effort into finding him.

- Thank you Sarah... I will not take any more of your time. I am really grateful for everything you told me.

- No problem Hayley. Here's my number so if you ever need anything…

- Actually… there is one more thing. In my dream you cast a spell on my house so vampires could not enter without an invitation. Can you do that?

- I can and I already have.

- What? When?

- When you were in a hospital and Leah contacted me for the first time. She sent me here to cast the spell.

- That's great, thank you.

- No problem. Take care of yourself Hayley. And if you ever need anything, just let me know. I hope you'll find Liam someday.

Hayley closed the door behind Sarah and sat on the couch. Lexi sat right next to her, poking Hayley's elbow with her nose to encourage her to pet her.

- He's real, Lexi. - Hayley said with a smile, cuddling up to the dog - Liam is real, I just need to… Oh my god! What have you done?!

Hayley has just noticed the paw prints all over her rug and sofa. She picked the dog up and tried to carry her to the bathroom which was not easy as Lexi weighted nearly as much as Hayley.

- I hope you like water Lexi, otherwise you will not enjoy what I am about to do with you now.

Hayley finally finished reading Leah's journal which was fascinating and unbelievable. She was such a powerful and clever girl and was getting stronger with every new spell. She could heal animals and bring dead flowers back to life. By the time she was all grown up, she could kill with the power of her mind and heal people with a simple touch. At first, she was afraid of what she was and the power she had, after all, she was just a teenager. But as she grew older and learnt to control the magic, all of a sudden, nearly everything became possible. She was not afraid of anyone or anything, she had what she wanted and went wherever she wished to. She was truly unstoppable and invincible. She mentioned Liam and Isabella many times and wrote about all the fun they had as children and how much they cared about each other. They spent many years together, travelling around the world and discovering different cultures. Leah was thinking about turning into a vampire but she was a witch, she wanted to join her ancestors in the afterlife and she didn't know where she would go as a vampire. She had a beautiful life, full of adventures and happiness, carefree and amazing. But one day, out of the blue, for no particular reason, she decided to take the ring off and start to grow old and that's were her journal ended. Hayley couldn't understand Leah's choice. *'Why did she choose to grow old and die? Why didn't she stay young forever? Why didn't she save herself with her magic? With all the power that she had she could have been anyone.'* Hayley looked at her ring and decided she would never take it off. That way, she could be with Liam forever without turning into a vampire. The only problem was that she had no idea where Liam was and she had no clue of where to find him.

Chapter 13

Liam woke up suddenly as if he had a terrible nightmare, short of breath and sweating. He looked at Isabella who was sitting by his bed looking angry and worried.

- Thank god you're finally awake. What the hell happened, Liam?

- I… I don't know… Where's Hayley?

- Who?

Liam sat on his bed confused, struggling to gather his thoughts.

- What happened, Isabella?

- I don't know. I came to you yesterday morning but you were still asleep. I tried to wake you up but you didn't react. I guessed there was some magic involved but I couldn't find a witch in this bloody town! There was one in Chicago but she was too busy to come over here... We were supposed to go to Miami, do you remember that? We talked about taking a trip.

- I remember that… But I thought it was last year…

- We spoke about it last month and then I went after my bounty.

Liam was trying to put all the pieces together. He looked pensive for another minute and then he smiled having realised what's happened.

- It's Leah.

- Leah? Our Leah?

- Yes, she put me into sleep.

- How? Why would she do that? What did you see?

- In my dream, I met a girl. She knew who I was and she loved me despite that. Eventually, she turned into a vampire and we were about to get married.

- Why would Leah show you that?

- She must be real. That girl. And Leah wants me to find her.

- Do you remember where you met her or what her full name was?

- Hayley Evans and we met in Aspen. I was in her house but now, I can't remember the address.

- Well, I really don't know what to think about it… But it's worth checking that Hayley Evans. I will have a look.

- Thank you, sister… It was amazing… I loved her so much. We were about to spend the whole eternity together. I was so happy with her.

- How do you know it was Leah?

- I saw her in my dream, right before I woke up. She knocked on my door and I opened. She approached me and gave me a hug. Then, she took my face in her warm soft hands and she said *'everything is going to be OK. You will find happiness again'* and then I woke up.

- Maybe, somehow, she found your true love? OK, I'll go now, search through the database and I'll come back to you as soon as I find anything. I'm so glad you're awake now. I was really worried about you.

Isabella left, leaving Liam alone with his thoughts. He truly believed that his best friend reached out to him from the grave to help him. She must have known, somehow, that he was unhappy and she wanted to help. *'So what is so special about that Hayley Evans that made Leah choose her? How could she know that Hayley would fall in love with me? And if she really exists, how do I approach her? What am I going to say? '* Liam had so many questions and no answers. He went to take a shower and had some breakfast. He has been asleep for two days and now he needed to go back to reality. He sat down at the kitchen table with a cup of coffee in his hands.

- I hope you know what you've done, Leah – he said aloud, looking at the empty sit in front of him – You can't mess with my head like that, you may leave me even more broken than I was so if Hayley is not real, I am going to be really angry with you, my dear friend.

He took a sip and looked around. *'So what do I do now?'* – he thought – *'How can I just go back to my old life, after what I've been through? I have nowhere to go, I have nothing to do... I can't write with all these thoughts running through my head, I can't sleep... I miss Hayley... And I miss Lexi... What a nice, unreal, made-up dog.'* – he smiled. Having nothing better to do, Liam turned his laptop on, googled *Aspen* and had a look at the street view of the city, moving his small orange man from one street to another, searching for a house he saw in his dream.

An hour later, Isabella stormed into Liam's house, letting the door slam loudly behind her.

- I found her! I found Hayley Evans in Aspen!

She handed the paper with all the details to Liam.

- Mrs Hayley Evans, thirty-four-year-old, widower, psychologist...That's her! Isabella, this is the girl!

- Great! – she yelled with excitement - Then pack your bags, we're going to Aspen.

Liam grabbed his phone, passport, wallet and jacket and started putting his shoes on.

- That's it? You're not taking anything else?

- I can buy anything else. Let's go.

They got into Isabella's car and started driving to O'Hare International Airport. They booked their evening flight over the phone to make sure there were two free seats available when they got to the airport.

- So, how are you feeling, brother? – Isabella glanced at Liam who looked pensive.

- Excited and nervous… She obviously doesn't know me. I already love her and she doesn't know anything

about me... I don't even know where I would start...
What will I say to her?

- Well, I think we can watch her from the distance for a
couple of days, make sure she doesn't have anyone and
you're not going to destroy her life with your sudden
appearance. Then, you can approach her at the store or a
park and just have a normal conversation about weather or
something. Something casual just to get her attention.
How did you two meet in your dream?

- She was attacked outside my window and I saved her.
I was honest with her from the very beginning and she
accepted me because I saved her life and she knew she
could trust me.

- If you want, I can attack her and you can save her and
we'll see if that works.

- I hope you're not serious, Isabella. I can't do that, I
can't put her through all that stress... We need to figure
something out. Although... I don't know if I can do that...
You have no idea how much she means to me. I can't
mess it up, I have only one chance and I need to do this
right.

- Don't stress too much about it, Liam. There must be a
good reason why Leah picked her. You obviously are
meant to be together so I don't think you can mess it up...
Maybe Leah showed you in her dreams too?

- I doubt that. She can't just reach out to anyone, there
must be a connection.

- So what's her connection to you?

- This bracelet.

It was a thin leather bracelet with a small silver charm,
a symbol of infinity.

- She gave me this before she left. – he continued - She
said she could use it to contact me if I ever needed her.

- She didn't give me anything.

- Well, it looks like she loved me more.

They both smiled.

- We'll figure something out, don't worry Liam. If it's meant to be, will be.

- I hope you're right.

They reached the airport right in time for their three-hour flight to Aspen. Isabella was reading a book, perfectly relaxed and Liam was trying to find the right words he would say to Hayley when they finally meet. He couldn't wait to see her and yet, the idea of meeting her was making him nervous. How could he approach the woman of his life, his true love? What would he say to her? Whatever came to his mind, didn't seem right. Maybe he should give it some more time. Maybe meeting her now was not a good idea. He looked at Isabella sleeping with her head tilted towards the window and a book loosely sitting on her lap. *'I wish I could switch off just like that'* – he thought and then gently took Isabella's book and started to read, although he did it so mindlessly that if someone had asked him what he'd read he wouldn't be able to repeat a single line.

- So, do you know what you will say to her? – asked Isabella as they were eating their breakfast at The Little Nell hotel.

- No, I imagined this so many times and still nothing feels right.

- Then let's just watch her for a day, you don't have to approach her today. Whenever you're ready, you'll find the right moment.

- You're right, I don't have to do anything, we can just watch her for a bit. Even if Leah is right thinking that Hayley is perfect for me, if she has someone, I won't do anything. It'd kill me to see her with another guy, but if she's happy with someone else... I won't break any good relationship she may already have.

- There will be time to make more decisions but now let's just take the first step and let's go to see her.

They got into the car they've rented at the airport and drove to the address Isabella got from the database. The West Bleeker Street was a nice neighbourhood, with each house surrounded by a short fence and tall trees decorated in the golden colours of autumn. They parked across the street and watched Hayley through the window. She was with some young girl, both sitting in the living room, Hayley with a notepad in her hand and the girl crying, constantly wiping the tears from her face with a white tissue.

- That's probably one of her clients – said Liam - Hayley's a psychologist.

They watched her for a couple of minutes.

- I can't sit here all day like a creep, staring at her through the window – said Liam annoyed and restless.

- Maybe we can go back in the afternoon when she's not working any more.

Suddenly, the front door opened and Hayley's client left. Without closing the door, Hayley put her jacket and shoes on, took her dog on a leash and also left the house.

- This is it. This is your chance Liam, go to her. – said Isabella gently pushing Liam out of the car.

- Alright... Go back to the hotel Isabella, I will follow her and see where she's going. Maybe I'll figure something out, play it by ear.

- Good luck.

Liam took a deep breath, got out of the car quietly and slowly started following Hayley, keeping a reasonable distance. He followed her to the Wagner Park. She let the dog off the leash and sat on the bench nearby. He watched her for a few minutes, walking back and forth. *'OK, I'll talk to her now... But what am I going to say? No, I can't do it, my head is completely empty, I need more time to think this through... No, I'll talk to her now.'* He decided to sit on the same bench and start a casual conversation just like Isabella suggested, hoping he wouldn't say anything stupid to scare her away.

- Hi – he said with a smile and sat down.

Hayley couldn't believe her own eyes. It was him, the man from her dreams, the one she loved and missed so much. *'He's here! O my god he's here! He knows me! No... how could he? Leah isn't related to him so she couldn't get into his head like she did with me so he can't possibly know. So why would he approach me? Why would he appear in front of me just like that if he didn't know? For god's sake, Leah! Why it all has to be so complicated with you?! Why didn't you give me any answers?! Oh my god, I need to say something, it's been far too long and I didn't say anything, I can't let him leave!'*

- Hi – she replied with a smile.

'Let's see what he has to say, let's put the ball in his court, it's much safer that way. I may say something stupid.'

- Which dog is yours?

- The black one. Lexi.

'Same name but a different dog' – thought Liam – *'why would the dog look different but Hayley looks exactly the same?'*

- Lexi is a very nice name. And what is yours?

- I'm Hayley. *'So he doesn't know me after all'.*

- Nice to meet you Hayley. I'm Liam.

Their handshake lasted longer than a usual one. They looked at each other smiling.

'God, I missed you so much! – thought Hayley – *I wish I could just put my arms around you and kiss you.'*

- It's a very nice ring you have.

- Thank you. It's magical. *'Ah, what the hell, let's see what he has to say about that.'*

- Really? What does it do? - Liam looked genuinely intrigued. *'Does she really think it's magical? Is it Leah's ring? If so then how did she get it?'*

- It makes me forever young.

- And do you really believe that?

- Of course, I believe in magic, don't you? I believe that this world is too big for humans only. There must be something more.

- Like what?

- I don't know… witches, vampires, werewolves, mermaids, aliens, ghosts…

- That's a very impressive list. – Liam smiled.

- Apparently, I am from a bloodline of witches.

- Are you really?

- Yes.

- Are you a witch too?

- No, I'm not.

- You say it as if you regretted it.

- Well, I think it would be cool to be something more than just a human… I think life without magic is boring and sad.

- So, if you met a creature from your list, what would you do?

- I would like to know everything about them. Get to know them.

They sat in silence for a minute, looking at Lexi chasing a Jack Russel. As that dog was much smaller, it was much quicker than Lexi which was clearly making her annoyed as she started to bark.

- So Liam, do you live nearby?

- No, I'm not from Aspen, but I plan on moving.

- Why Aspen?

Liam smiled and shrugged his shoulders.

- I don't know… I just have a good feeling about this place. What about you?

- I lived in Aspen my whole life and I like it here.

- Aren't you tired of the weather?

- Not really, I like snow and the cold. Besides, I love skiing so there is no better place for someone like me.

Another brief moment of silence.

- What about you Liam? Do you believe in magic?

- I do. Like you said, the universe is too big and there must be something more than just people.

Lexi came to them all wet and dirty, weaving her tail and jumping around. She approached Liam and put her front paws on his lap, leaving dirty prints on his jeans.

- Lexi stop it! I'm so sorry, Liam, I am still trying to teach her to behave. I need to go home now. – she put the dog back on the leash - Will I see you again?

- Definitely. It was nice to meet you, Hayley.

- Likewise.

They shook their hands again and Hayley left, leaving Liam on the bench alone. She was walking away fast, pulled by the dog. Liam was watching her, until she disappeared around the corner.

'I should have asked her for her number. How could I be so stupid? I should have asked her on a date..' Liam wanted to follow Hayley home but he was afraid it might scare her away so instead, he went slowly back to the hotel. He didn't pay any attention to the weather or people passing him by. Although it was sunny, it was cold and the temperature seemed the same in the sun as it was in the shade. The cold wind brushed Liam's bare neck and made him shiver. He put the collar up, put his hands deeply into his pockets and sped up. He didn't prepare well for his trip to Aspen so by the time he got to the hotel, even though it was only a five-minute walk, he was already cold to the bone.

- And? How did it go? Did you talk to her? – asked Isabella the moment Liam opened the door.

She was reading a book, sitting on the perfectly white sheets, having her duvet rolled behind her back.

- I did. – he went straight for the kettle and was glad the water inside was already freshly boiled. He reached for the mug and made himself a cup of tea to warm up.

- What did she say? Did she recognise you? – Isabella was getting annoyed by the fact that Liam didn't say everything at once but waited for her to ask every single question.

- No, she acted as if we didn't know each other. She was very nice and friendly and wearing Leah's ring.

- Really? So maybe she has a connection to her like you do? Maybe Leah contacted her too?

Liam sat down in the armchair, with his coat still on and a cup of tea in his hands.

- Well, she said something about having witches in her family and that the ring was magical, but it's hard to tell whether she really believes that or she was just trying to make an interesting conversation. Maybe I should go to her…

- It looks like she doesn't know you… Or maybe is pretending just like you… Are you ready to take the risk?

Liam thought for a minute before he replied.

- I think I am. Just like you said if it's meant to be, will be and I can't mess it up. She likes me, it's easy to tell I just need to find out if she knows anything. There is a small chance that Leah reached out to her as well, she could have done it through that ring.

- Then go to her and see.

- But what will I say? That I followed her home?

- No, you definitely can't say that… Maybe… Maybe have a walk in her neighbourhood and you can just bump into each other somewhere on the street.

- That may work actually. I bet she'll take her dog for another walk later today.

- I bet she will.

- OK, I will take the car, park in a reasonable distance from her house and wait until she's out again. I'll just grab something to eat and buy a coat because it's freezing out there!

\- I told you to pack.

Liam smiled, grabbed the car keys and left.

Liam was sitting in a car down the street, a few houses from Hayley's house. He was eating his chicken tortilla and gazing at Hayley's front door every now and then. Even though it was quite cold outside and winter has started decorating the streets with the first large snowflakes, Liam was ready to sit in that car for hours, waiting for a perfect moment. He was no longer cold in his brand-new woollen sweater he grabbed an hour earlier and his pleasantly warmed up Hyundai Kona. He took a sip of his Earl Grey and sighed.

\- Come on Hayley, time for a walk.

He wanted to go to her and just tell her everything but he knew it would be a stupid thing to do. He needed to be patient and wait. He reached for his cell phone and googled Hayley's name. On her website, there was a schedule her clients could use to book their appointments without a need to call Hayley directly, especially that she couldn't answer her phone during her working hours. Liam entered today's date and noticed the appointments went through from eight in the morning to six in the evening, with only a ninety-minute window that Hayley has already used that morning for her walk to the park.

\- So she won't come out until six then – said Liam to himself – No point to linger here then.

He turned the key and drove back to the hotel.

At six in the evening, Liam was back in a car, parked near Hayley's house, waiting impatiently for her to leave the house. *I should have bought some perfumes... and brush my teeth. What the hell was I thinking? I'm trying to make a good impression looking like this.'* He sighed loudly, moved his feet nervously and played with his fingers. Quarter after six, the front door finally opened and Hayley left the house with Lexi by her side. Liam took a deep breath *'OK, here we go'*. He crossed the street and sped up, making sure he's ahead of Hayley, which was easy to do as Lexi was stopping every few steps to sniff. When he was about twenty meters ahead, he crossed the street again and started casually walking back, with his hands in his pockets. When he was only a few meters away, he stopped and smiled but Hayley was deep in thought, not paying any attention to him.

- Hi – he said with the greatest smile.

- Hi! Liam, right? – Hayley was genuinely surprised to see him. She was so sure the next time they'd meet would be in the park again.

- Good to see you again. So do you live nearby?

- Yes, just a bit further down the street… Would you like to come in for a cup of tea? It's such a cold evening and it looks like it's started snowing again.

- Sure, that would be nice, thank you.

They started slowly walking back.

- Sorry Lexi – said Haley petting her dog – We'll go out again tomorrow, now it's time to go home.

- Let's postpone that tea and take your dog for a proper walk. I think we're both properly dressed so the weather won't be a problem.

- Are you sure?

- Of course, Lexi was home all day, she deserves a bit of freedom.

- Very well then. Let's go.

They turned around and started slowly walking ahead, letting Lexi choose the direction.

- So tell me something about yourself – started Liam.

- Well… I'm a psychologist, I have twin sisters April and June and I like skiing… I don't know what else I can tell you, there is not much to say.

- What about that magical ring? Where did you get it?

- I inherited it recently. It's passed through generations and until now, I didn't even know I had witches in my family. I must say it's very exciting and fascinating and wearing this ring makes me feel invincible and unique.

- I think you're very unique even without the ring.

- What makes you say that?

- I… I just wanted to give you a complement.

- Right... Thank you. What about you? What can you tell me about yourself?

- I'm a writer, I have a sister Isabella and I am about to move to Aspen so if you know which neighbourhood is the best, I'm happy to consider some recommendations.

- This one. It's very quiet and safe and walking distance from the park and shops but I don't think anyone is selling a house nearby… You know what? I recently read a journal about a sibling called Liam and Isabella. How strange is that?

- Well, these are very common names.

- Right…

They walked in silence for a few minutes but it didn't make them feel uncomfortable. They enjoyed each other's company even with no single word being said. It was just nice to be together again.

- Do you still want that tea – asked Hayley when they reached her house again.

- Sure.

- Great! Come in – she added when she opened the door, remembering that Liam wouldn't be able to enter the house without an invitation.

She quickly cleaned Lexi's paws and headed to the kitchen.

- So what was the journal about? What did you find out about that other Liam and Isabella – asked Liam as he was sitting down at the table.

Hayley quickly brewed the tea and sat down opposite to him.

- Well… it was a pair of vampires. They lived back in the eighteenth century and they were close friends of my ancestor Leah. And maybe I don't know you but I think you and that Liam from the journal are very much alike.

- What makes you say that?

- Well… you're both nice and friendly. You both enjoy writing and I bet you care deeply about your family and friends too.

- It sounds like me indeed. *'She knows it's me, I can feel it. Hayley I know wouldn't let a complete stranger into her house, but she invited me because I'm not a stranger. She read the journal and she knows who I am. That's why Leah was so sure we two would get along.'* What if I told you I am that Liam from the journal, what would you do?

'He's going to tell me the truth that it's really him. I see he wants me to know, he wants to be honest with me.'

- I would be happy because I have so many questions for that Liam.

- What about the vampire bit? Doesn't it scare you?

- Not at all. But I would need a proof, I couldn't just believe in magic without seeing any.

Liam let his eyes turn black just for a second but Hayley noticed that.

- I think that was my proof then – she said with a smile.

She wasn't scared or confused so Liam sighed with relief.

- I must say you took it pretty well. Other people tend to freak out.

- I'm not like other people.

- Yes, I think we have already established that. So, what questions do you have for me then? Because now it's obvious I am your Liam from the journal.

- If you're that Liam than I think I already know everything about you. I mentioned the questions just to encourage you to give me the proof. The truth is that I know you inside out already.

- Do you really? How come? Was that much information in that journal?

- No, but I had a dream about you. A very realistic one.

- Really? That's very interesting because I got the feeling that I know everything about you too.

- OK… Let's check. What do you know?

- You love the smell of freshly cut grass.

Hayley snorted – and who doesn't? That doesn't proof anything.

- You watch comedies only as you think life is too sad and too scary already so you don't want to see any dramas or horrors. You are very sentimental and even though I didn't have a look around your house, I guess you have photos of your family and friends all the way up the stairs.

- Maybe…

- You think that Lord of the Rings is the greatest movie ever made, you're good at racing games but really suck in football.

- How could you possibly know that? – Hayley was truly surprised.

- I just do. So in your magical dream… did you, by any chance, go to Miami and Hawaii with me? Did you jump off the cliff and swim in the ocean? Did you go to the ball?

Hayley started having tears in her eyes.

- So Leah messed with your head too, huh?

Liam approached Hayley and kissed her without hesitation.

- I'm so happy I found you.

They spent a few minutes holding each other in their arms and then ended up talking about their dreams and how similar they were. They talked about Leah and Lexi and what has happened since they both woke up. The only difference was that Hayley's dream ended up with a massacre in the woods and Liam's with Leah visiting him in his house but Hayley didn't tell Liam about her ending. She thought he didn't need to know. She was never going to do what she's done in her dream so she decided that single detail could remain unsaid.

Liam woke up early in the morning and looked at Hayley sleeping by his side. He smiled and brushed her hair off her face. She opened her eyes and smiled.
- Good morning.
- Good morning. Did you sleep well?
- Very.
- I missed you so much.
- I missed you too.
- So, what's the plan, Liam? Are you moving to Aspen?
- Definitely. I can work wherever so there is nothing in Rockford that I should go back to.
- What about Isabella?
- She's at the hotel now. I didn't come back last night so I assume she figured out I'm with you.
- Call her. Let her meet me.
- Just remember that Leah didn't create any dream for her so whatever you think you two went through, never really happened.
- I know. I'll pretend that I don't know her, like I pretended I didn't know you.
- Yes, you played your part quite well, I wasn't sure whether you knew me or not.
- You too. It was really hard to guess how much you knew. OK, it's time to get up – Hayley got out of bed and

stretched - It's Lexi's breakfast time. I bet she's angry with me for keeping the bedroom door closed.

She opened the door and let the dog in. Lexi gave Hayley the look meaning she was not very happy. She passed her by and went straight to Liam, sniffing his feet.

- I'm glad she likes you, she's not very friendly with strangers.

Liam reached out his hand and petted the dog.

- She's different from the one Leah showed me in my dream but I must say this one is even better.

- She must have understood what you said – said Hayley seeing Lexi wagging her tail. – Come on Lexi! Time for breakfast!

- Hi, come in. – said Hayley when Isabella showed up at the door.

- Hi, it's nice to finally meet you. You have no idea how much I've heard about you.

- Good things I hope.

- Only.

They all sat in the living room. Hayley brought some tea and biscuits. It was good to see Isabella again but she needed to remember that the past they once shared was now gone and they were nothing but strangers.

- You have a very lovely house. – said Isabella having looked around - It looks nothing like what me or Liam has.

- Thank you. Well, I spent every day in here and you are a guest in your own house, being on the road nearly all the time. Plus you change your house every decade or so, so I bet it's difficult to feel attached to something you know you're going to leave behind one day. I've lived here nearly all my adult life and I love this place.

- Right, I forgot that you probably know everything about me by now. To be honest... It's weird talking to you knowing that you know… The only other person who knew was Leah but she was a witch and you're just a human… Sorry, it didn't come out right.

- No, that's fine, I get it. At least you can be yourself around me and you don't have to tiptoe, afraid you may say or do something that would scare me away.

- So what do you know about Leah? What is her connection to you?

- I haven't really met her, she didn't show herself in my dream. But I think I know her pretty well now, after I've read her journal. She was my ancestor and all her stuff was given to me. I have the journal and the ring – Hayley showed Isabella the emerald ring – She mentioned you and Liam too, she really loved you like a sister.

- I loved her too. – Isabella smiled nostalgically – I really miss her. Maybe she'll come to me in my dreams one day. It would be nice to have her around again, she was so much fun.

- Sister – Liam interrupted - I decided to move to Aspen. There is nothing for me in Rockford and Hayley has her sisters and her clients here so it would be inconvenient for her to move.

- Oh… Right… Yes, that sounds reasonable.

- What about you? Will you move too?

Isabella looked down at the biscuit she was holding in her hand, thinking what to say. She didn't expect that question at all, at least not so soon.

- I… I think I will give you two some time together and stay in Illinois for a little longer.

- Sure, if that's what you want.

Liam didn't mind. He loved his sister but a few months or years apart didn't mean that much compared to the eternity they had ahead of them. She spent enough of her time worrying and taking care of her big brother and she needed a break and think about herself for a change.

- Isabella, you don't have to do this. - Hayley said - I don't want you two to separate because of me. We can figure something out if you don't want to move to Aspen.

- You get it the wrong way, Hayley. I know I can move here anytime, but I also think that Liam should spend some time around other people, not just me. We can always call or visit, it's not like we'll never see each other again so don't worry, it's not a big deal.

Isabella got up.

- Thank you for the tea but I'll be going now. Hayley, it was really nice to meet you. Liam, I will check out and return the car. I will fly home this evening.

- I'll fly with you. I need to take care of the house and organise the moving.

- OK, I will reserve two tickets then. Bye Hayley. Till we meet again?

- Till we meet again.

Hayley and Liam took Lexi for a walk to the park, grabbed a takeaway and spent the rest of the day at home. Liam didn't have to leave until six so they decided that a quiet evening at home was exactly what they needed before they parted again.

- I need to start looking for a house nearby. – said Liam lying in bed squeezed between Hayley and Lexi.

- Why won't you move in with me? I know that we have just met yesterday, but technically, we are engaged.

- Are you sure about this?

- Of course. Why wouldn't I be? I love you.

- And what about that engagement? Do you still want to get married?

- Absolutely! Do you?

- I do.

Hayley sadly looked at the ticking clock and sighed. It was their last few minutes before Liam had to go.

- Hayley… Did you think about your transition?
- I thought about it but I have mixed feelings. I'm not sure it's such a good idea.
- Do you remember what you said when we had that conversation in our dream?
- That I regretted not making that decision earlier. I know, I remember what I said and how I felt. I also remember how disappointed I was when I woke up and realised I was human again. But I need to give it another thought. It is a tough decision to make.
- Hm…
- What?
- To be honest, I didn't expect you to hesitate.
- Really? So you think I should do it?
- I can't tell you what to do, Hayley.
- I know, but I want to know your opinion.
Liam sat on the bed and looked at Hayley.
- I think you should do it. I remember how I felt when I thought you were going to die. I remember the fear of losing you from the day we met till the moment you turned. I was afraid every day that it was going to be our last day and I may not see you tomorrow. I remember how relieved I was when you finally made that decision, but it has to be your own choice and you should not do this just for me.
- Let me think about it and I will let you know next time you're here.
- Very well. – Liam looked at the clock and sighed - I have to go now. Unfortunately, it's nearly six and Isabella will be here any minute.
Liam got up, dressed and kissed Hayley goodbye.
- I will take care of everything as fast as I can so hopefully I'll be back next weekend.
- I already miss you.
- I love you.
- I love you too.

When Liam left, Hayley stayed in bed and a feeling of sadness and loneliness began to emerge. She whistled and smiled hearing Lexi running up the stairs. The dog jumped on the bed and licked Hayley's face and wagged her tail.

- I'm so glad I have you Lexi. – she said cuddling up to Lexi's soft fur - You can always cheer me up.

The dog jump off the bed and barked looking at Hayley clearly wanting her to react.

- I get it, you want to go for a walk?

Lexi barked again and ran down the stairs. Hayley got up and took her dog for a fast-paced walk around the neighbourhood. It was a cold November evening and the traces of the first snow were still covering the ground with a thin white layer. The wind brought an intense smell of a gingerbread latte from a nearby café. Hayley smiled looking at the snowflakes that suddenly started to fall. The falling snow made her feel as if she was inside a snow globe. Lexi was trying to catch the falling snowflakes but they were melting instantly in her mouth.

- If you like snow, you will love it tomorrow when the whole garden is covered in a thick layer.

They jogged through the snow and came back home all wet. Hayley dried Lexi with a towel she kept by the front door. She made sure her paws were clean before she let her into the living room. She made herself a mug of hot chocolate with raspberries and vanilla ice cream and slipped under the blanket on the sofa with Lexi by her side. Hayley was staring at the dog slowly falling asleep with her head on Hayley's lap. She was thinking about that big decision she needed to make by the next weekend. She put the mug down and reached for a notepad which she kept by the sofa and started writing all pros and cons that came to her mind.

- OK, so, pros of me turning into a vampire… Let's see… I can be with Liam forever. I will never grow old or get sick and I could give Leah's ring to my sisters… I won't be so vulnerable anymore... OK, cons... Blood didn't seem an issue in my dream so I think this is something I could get used to so I won't put it on the list. So, first con - I would have to move every few years... and I would have to stay away from my sisters.

By writing that list Hayley realised there were not that many cons, but it would be difficult to leave her sisters and never see them again. They have grown closer since Hayley left the hospital and the twins visited every Sunday and called a few times a week with any news they had and to check up on Hayley. How could she leave them now? Hayley was thinking hard trying to figure out the right way.

- I have to tell them the truth. They need to know everything and that way we could still see each other. No lies, no secrets... That's the only way.

She decided she would talk to April and June the next day. She would be completely honest with them, hoping they would understand and accept her decision. It would be very difficult to bring the twins into that magical world, making them aware of all the impossible things that were real but she needed to give it a go. She couldn't become a vampire without making sure her sisters would still love her and accept her.

She put the notepad down and reached for her hot chocolate again. *'They'll understand, they are smart girls and they love me and care about me and they will want the best for me. I just need to make sure I bring this up the right way. I just need to find the right words.'*

Hayley woke up early the next day although she didn't expect April and June until eleven. She got up and let Lexi out into the garden which was all covered in snow as she expected. It was snowing heavily throughout the night. Lexi was jumping around as if the snow was burning her paws. She was barking at the snowflakes and Hayley didn't know whether she was having fun or was annoyed. Either way, the way Lexi was acting made her laugh.

- You are such a silly dog, it's just snow and you're not a puppy anymore. Come back home, it's freezing!

But the dog didn't want to come back, being far too intrigued by that white, wet and cold thing that was quickly turning into water in her mouth.

- Fine, stay here but I'm closing the door so you're on your own.

Lexi looked at Hayley just for a moment before coming back to barking and digging in the snow. Hayley put a few more logs into the fireplace and sat on the sofa with a cup of tea, still in her thick and soft pyjamas and fluffy winter socks. She took a few deep breaths looking at the growing flames. *'Everything is going to be OK. I can do this. They are my sisters and they love me. Worst case scenario, they'll think I'm crazy and they'll lock me away'* – she smiled and took a sip of her tea.

- Hi sister. It's so nice outside. Look at that snow! – said April shaking the snow off and making way for June.

- Hi, yes I know. Lexi is still in the garden.

- So, how have you been, Hayley?

- Actually, there is something specific I wanted to talk about with you two.

She got up and brought Leah's journal along with Eleonora's letter and the letter from the solicitor. Twins looked at her with interest.

- A few weeks ago, I received a letter from a solicitor saying that our aunt passed away and I was mentioned in her will.

- Who passed away?

- Eleonora Stone, she was our mother's cousin from Alaska.

- I've never heard of her.

- Me neither, but obviously she knew about us.

- Why didn't she visit then?

- No idea. She didn't say anything about it in her letter.

Hayley handed over both letters so her sisters could read them carefully.

- Have you read that journal, Hayley?

- Yes I have. It's quite interesting. Apparently, some members of our family were witches.

April and June laughed but Hayley didn't.

- You can't be serious Hayley. Do you really believe that?

- I do.

- How can you believe that? It's just some very old book, written by someone with a very vivid imagination.

- I want you to have this journal and read it. And I want you to be open-minded.

Hayley's sisters looked at her confused. It was difficult to understand why their big sister started believing in magic, all of a sudden, after reading some old journal sent by a complete stranger.

- I will summarise it for you – Hayley continued even though she was slowly losing her confidence - It was written by a teenage girl who has just found out she's a witch. She put in there everything that she has learnt and something about herself and her friends and life in general, what it looked like in the eighteenth century.

April and June were listening carefully. They looked genuinely interested now so Hayley continued.

- She also wrote about her two best friends Liam and Isabella who have been turned into vampires.

- Wait – April looked at her with disbelieve - so it's not only about witches but also vampires? Wow, Hayley, I can't believe you think it's real. It's bananas!

- I know how it sounds and that it's hard for you to believe it but it is true.

The twins looked at Hayley a bit nervous, worried that the suicide attempt messed with her head and now their big sister was slowly losing her mind.

- I met Liam. – added Hayley believing it was her last chance to make the twins believe her. '*It can't get any worse at this point. They think I'm mental already so all I need right now it a proof. The journal means nothing but if they met Liam, that would be something.*'

- Liam? The vampire from the book?

- Yes, and Isabella too.

They looked at Hayley shocked. Now they were sure Hayley was going insane but they decided to be careful, not to hurt her feelings.

- And are they really vampires?

- They are.

- How can you know that?

- They proved it to me.

- Where did you meet them? When? How did that happen?

- Well, it's a bit more complicated and it's a story for some other time. I don't want to give you too much information at once and I think I have already told you too much. I should have let you read that journal first.

- So let me get this right... - said June furrowing her brow - You received a book, a journal that was written by our ancestor who claimed to be a witch... and you met people she mentioned in that journal who lived in the eighteenth century and are now vampires?

'*And how am I supposed to answer now?*' - thought Hayley, slowly giving up – *They don't believe me, I can see they think I'm completely going insane.*'

- Yes, exactly. - she finally responded, with a note of resignation in her voice.

- OK, – said April, trying not to make Hayley feel bad - we will read the journal and we will talk about it next time, OK?

- Sure. I think that would be better.

- And what about the ring? Do you have it?

Hayley showed the ring to her sisters.

- Wow. It's beautiful. That must be worth something for sure!

- Probably, but I don't want to sell it. It was in our family for generations so let's keep it that way.

The twins didn't say anything more so Hayley got up and let Lexi in. The dog was very happy to see April and June as she loved playing with them.

- Oh my god! Hayley she's all wet!

Hayley took the dog and dried her with the towel, letting her lay down by the fireplace. After that, the girls changed the subject and did not go back to talking about the journal anymore.

Hayley enjoyed her Sunday meetings with April and June. At first, they didn't have much to talk about but now it was easy to discuss whatever was going on in their lives. Hayley decided to leave some facts out for now so she didn't mention being engaged to Liam and planning on turning into a vampire. She needed the twins to read the journal first so they had a bit of a background and then, she would introduce Liam and tell them everything else they needed to know. It was a lot of information to process and the most important part now was for them to believe that everything described in that journal was one hundred percent real. But the look on their faces made Hayley realised that it was not going to be easily done.

Hayley spent the whole week preparing for Liam to move in. She made some space in the wardrobe for his clothes and bought an extra pillow and duvet knowing that he was not going to bring those from Illinois. She also bought a large bookcase as Liam was selling his house with all furniture. All he was about to bring with him was just some clothes, documents and an enormous number of books and journals that he has collected throughout his long life. Hayley also directed some of her clients to her colleagues so she could have more free time. She talked with Liam every day, starting in the evening and finishing at dawn, leaving Hayley sometimes with only two or even one hour of sleep, before she had her first client. April and June called a few times but didn't mention the journal even once and Hayley decided not to push.

Liam arrived on Saturday afternoon. His stuff was still on its way and was supposed to be delivered on Monday. They ordered a takeaway and spent their Saturday evening at home, watching movies and dancing in the living room.

- Having a good time, Hayley? – asked Liam as they were slowly swinging in the dark room, gently illuminated by the dying out fire.

- Yes I am.

Liam reached out to his pocket and showed Hayley the ring.

- You already agreed to marry me but I thought it would be nice to have an engagement ring for real, not only in your dreams.

He put the ring on Hayley's finger. It was exactly the same one she got from him in the woods by the river.

- It's very beautiful, thank you. But like I said before, with or without the ring I would still marry you… Liam, I need you to know that I have spoken with my sisters and I told them about Leah. I gave them her journal to read.

Liam looked surprised.

- And what did they say?

- Well… they think I'm crazy.

- Can you blame them? It's hard to start believing in magic just like that. To be honest with you… I am still wondering how Leah knew that you would like me? That you wouldn't freak out like everyone else.

- Well... I am a psychologist, I don't jump to conclusion, I don't judge. I try to gather all information before I comment on anything and I try to understand the way the others think. I assume Leah knew how open-minded I was and that I would give you a chance.

- And your sisters are not like you, are they?

- No. But nevertheless, I needed them to know because... I decided I would turn and I can't just leave my sisters because of that. They mean too much to me.

- That's great! What made you decide?

- I thought about all pros and cons and saw that the biggest con is the fact that I would have to lie to my sisters and leave them before they noticed something changed. But if they knew the truth, I wouldn't have to leave.

- Well, I hope you'll have more luck with your sisters than I had with other people in the past.

They turned off the music and turned on TV preparing for an evening marathon.

- Were you really married once? – asked Hayley as she was bringing the popcorn and coca cola from the kitchen.

- I was. But it was a very long time ago and there is nothing more to say. So, when are your sisters coming over?

- Tomorrow around eleven.

- OK, I will go out before that. Maybe I could take Lexi with me for a long walk.

- Actually, I need you to be here. I want them to meet you so you can prove I am not crazy... but now I think it's a good idea for you to take Lexi out so I can talk to them first and then you can join us... It would be better that way.

- I'll do whatever you want Hayley and I'll leave it completely up to you how you want to deal with your sisters. Just remember that people are afraid of vampires, of everything that is unknown and unexplainable to be exact and they may freak out.

- I know my sisters Liam and I know how to handle them. Everything will be OK, trust me. They are descendants of a witch so they are not like other people. As a matter of fact, I'm afraid one of them may be a witch. Someone told me it's possible but I'm afraid to test that theory. First, we need to sort out you and me, then, we can check if any of them is a witch. Everything in right time.

- So I assume I cannot talk to them about being a witch then. Tell me something about them so I know what I can talk about.

- Let's see… April is more reserved and introverted and may not make a good first impression but she's very sweet and lovely and caring once you get to know her. She loves painting and she's really good at it. She's going to have her paintings auctioned next week and she's very excited about it. You can talk to her about that.

- OK… and April is the one with long hair?

- That's right. June is more talkative and easy-going. She doesn't really have any hobbies but she loves to party so you can talk to her about going out, dancing, karaoke and plans for a Friday night. She's very easy to talk to.

- Does she play any sports?

- Not really.

- Hm… for a girl who doesn't play any sports, she has a lot of sports clothes. Every photo of her that you ever showed me presents her in sweats and t-shirts. No dresses or skirts like April.

- Despite being twins, they are quite different. But they get along fine and love spending time together. April is the more reasonable one so I know she can take care of June if needed. But June is fun and I know she can keep April entertained. Obviously they need each other.

- OK, so… painting… karaoke… partying. Got it. I am ready to talk to them.

- I know you are. I'm just worried they are not quite ready to talk to you.

- Don't worry Hayley. Worst case scenario they will never visit you again and try to stay away from me. But good part is that you'll have everything in twos: two birthday parties, two thanksgivings and Christmases.

- Like a kid of a divorced couple.

- Exactly.

- That's not funny Liam.

- Do they drink? I bet it would be easier to pass that information when they're both drunk, relaxed and having a good time.

- I'm not going to make my little sisters drunk. We'll have that conversation like adults.

- Sober, tense and anxious? – Liam added with a gentle smile.

- Exactly.

On Sunday morning Hayley woke up with anxiety. She was stressed about the conversation she was about to have with her sisters. The way they looked at her last time and the fact they didn't mention that journal even once yet was not very promising. She was afraid that despite the witchy blood in their veins, they may still react like every other normal human and they may simply panic. She sighed loudly, got up, took Lexi and went jogging to clear her mind. It was not snowing that morning, the sky was perfectly blue and the sun was reflecting on the snow. Although there were already quite a few centimetres of snow lying on the ground, the pavements were cleared and gritted.

- Good morning. - Liam greeted Hayley with a smile as she walked through the door with her face red from the frosty air - Are you feeling better now?

- Not really. I am surprised how stressed I am.

- I am sure everything is going to be OK. They are your sisters and they love you very much.

- Don't go too far with Lexi. I plan on talking to them right away so I think you can give us fifteen minutes and then come back.

- Are you sure it's enough?

- Definitely. I need you here for them to believe me, because it doesn't matter what I tell them, they need to see some proof.

- Very well then. I'll be back quarter past eleven. Unless something changes, call me.

He put his shoes on and Lexi on a leash – good luck – he added with a smile before he disappeared behind the closed door.

- So… have you read the journal? – Hayley cut to the chase as she sat down with the twins in the living room.

- Most of it, yes.

- And? What do you think?

- Well… - the girls looked at one another - Like we said before, we think it's just a book and nothing more. We don't believe a single word. I have never seen any proof of magic in my life and I have no reason to believe that it all could have been true. Sorry, Hayley I know you're disappointed and it's not what you expected to hear…

- No, I expected you wouldn't believe it. But… let's say, hypothetically, that it is real and witches and vampires really exist. What would you think of them?

- Depends on whether they were good or evil.

- What would you think of Leah, Isabella and Liam?

- I would say that they all seemed nice – June said - Leah saved a few people with her magic and the other two were trying very hard not to hurt anyone despite their nature. They seemed friendly, I would say. What about you April?

- I think the same. I mean… they haven't done anything wrong so how could we dislike them only because they were different from us?

- Good points. I think the same… So… - Hayley's heart was beating fast and her hands were getting sweatier and sweatier. She started playing nervously with her fingers, refraining from biting her nails - what would you do if I told you that Liam would be here shortly?

- Liam from the book?

- Yes, exactly the same Liam.

- The vampire?

- Yes.

- Well… I would say that you are insane and there is definitely something wrong with you. – April smiled thinking that Hayley was joking.

But she was clearly not. Hayley didn't laugh or smile, she didn't say anything, just looked at the twins, pensive.

- Hayley, are you serious about this? - June got a bit nervous - Will someone come over here?

Hayley noticed that both her sisters got serious now.

- Don't worry girls. He's very nice and charming and polite and you have absolutely no reason to be afraid of him. He's my friend. I've known him for a while.

The moment Hayley finished her sentence, Liam came in with Lexi. The girls looked at each other completely puzzled, absolutely unaware of what to expect. Till now, they were sure it was all in Hayley's head.

- Don't let her off the leash yet!

Hayley yelled and ran to clean Lexi's paws.

- How is it going? - Liam whispered to her ear.

- I think they are starting to believe me now.

They let Lexi say 'hello' to the girls first and then Hayley followed with Liam.

- Girls, this is Liam Anderson. Liam, these are April and June, my sisters.

- Nice to meet you. - Liam said with a smile - I have heard so much about you two.

Liam reached out his hand to greet them. They shook his hand without hesitation and sat down looking at him with interest. Hayley broke the silence.

- Liam, I told them about you and I think that the best way to prove that you are what you are would be to impress them with your speed. What do you think? Could you bring yourself a cup from the kitchen so I can pour you some coffee?

Liam got up, went to the kitchen and came back with a cup in his hands within two seconds. April and June were looking at him, paralysed, with their jaws down and eyes wide open.

- How did you… what…

- What the hell just happened?

June asked the question as April clearly couldn't make a full sentence.

- Do you believe me now, sisters? There are many other ways of proving that this is a real vampire but I thought the show of speed would be the best one. I am not insane and the journal I gave you was not just a book.

The girls stared at Liam until he finally began to blush, feeling uncomfortable being the centre of attention. April finally spoke.

- Are you a real vampire?

- Yes I am. Everything that you read in the journal really happened. Everything is true.

April and June looked at each other, trying to comprehend what was going on. What they have just seen made them believe in magic. It was unbelievable but real and they couldn't deny it. They didn't know what to say, they couldn't find any right words so Hayley decided to break the silence once again.

- Liam, could you please give us a moment alone?

- Of course.

Liam went to the kitchen with his regular human speed, leaving girls alone in the living room. Hayley knew he would hear every single word anyway but April and June didn't know that and she hoped they would feel more comfortable if he was not around.

- So? What do you think?

- Well - June started still glancing at the kitchen door - I believe you now. I mean… What I saw was very unbelievable… so I guess that magic is real after all.

- And you April?

- What if I cut myself by accident? Would he freak out?

Hayley smiled but April was seriously concerned.

- No, everything would be OK. This wouldn't be an issue. You are perfectly safe around him.

Hayley waited a few seconds waiting for more questions.

- So, are you two OK now? – she asked as the girls were not saying anything - Can I ask him to join us?

- Yeah, I think I'm OK – June replied - It still feels weird tough. I can't believe it's happening.

April just nodded and didn't say anything.

Hayley went to the kitchen.

- You can join us now.

Hayley decided to start a casual conversation with Liam so the girls didn't have to say anything.

- How was your walk with Lexi? Where did you go?

- We just had a walk around the neighbourhood. I assumed you would take her to the park this afternoon. The weather is great. I mean, it's a bit chilly but sunny.

- Yes, it's nice to finally enjoy the sun after a week of clouds and snow. What was the weather like in Rockford?

- It's a bit cold but not snowing. Feels more like autumn than winter.

- Where is Rockford?

June finally spoke. She was more relaxed now.

- About two-hour drive from Chicago.

- Illinois… never been there… So… how you two met if you're not from Aspen?

Hayley decided it was not the best time to tell them about the dream. They already had a lot of information to process.

- It's a long story for some other time.

- OK. Can't wait to hear all about it.

June was more relaxed and comfortable but April was still quiet so Liam decided to engage her in a conversation.

- So, April, I've heard that you put your paintings up for auction.

For a moment April hesitated with her answer but she didn't want to be rude especially with Liam being so nice.

- Yes. I advertised them online because the gallery is too expensive.

April reached for her cell phone and showed Liam her paintings.

- Wow. Very impressive. You are really good.

- Thank you.

- Can I buy this one?

Liam selected a painting presenting a Viking boat with an amazing red sunset in the background.

- Thank you, that's very nice of you but you don't have to do this.

- What are you talking about? This is an amazing painting and I wish to buy it from you.

- If you really like it, I can give it to you for free. You are Hayley's friend.

- Absolutely not. I want to support a young artist and I wish to pay for it. I will buy it online now and you can deliver it next Sunday when you come over again.

- Oh, OK, I will. Thank you very much Liam, that's very nice of you.

'That's going well' – thought Hayley – *'they are obviously tense and uneasy but they talk to him anyway,*

they didn't freak out and storm out of here and that's a good sign. I knew I could count on them. Wondering if it's because they don't want to upset me or it's that witchy blood running through their veins...'

They got through the dinner and desert without any unpleasant silence, able to talk about weather, Rockford, Aspen, dogs and New Year's Eve. Hayley saw every now and then how the girls watched Liam eating, clearly not listening what he was saying but being deep in thought.

- Time flies – said June getting up from the sofa - it's already seven o'clock. We should go now.

- Why? - Hayley asked surprised - There is no place you had to be so stay. We can watch a movie or something.

But Liam had a different idea.

- How about karaoke?

- I don't think Hayley would like to go. - April knew her sister too well and she was sure Hayley would pass.

- No, why? - Hayley got excited - I think it's a great idea. Let's go.

- But you will have to sing.

- I'll sing. We all will.

- OK then, karaoke it is.

They went to the nearby bar and managed to still get on the list but there was no time for all three girls to sing separately so they decided to sing together. They had fun listening to others and quietly laughed at those who didn't sound that good. The place was a bit crowded but quiet as people didn't want to disturb those ones who were on the stage.

- Hayley, have you ever sung before? - June asked.

Hayley was about to say 'yes' but then realised that the only time she participated in karaoke was in her dream, so technically she has never done karaoke before.

- No, I haven't but it looks fun so I want to do this.

It was fun night indeed. Liam sang Pour Some Sugar On Me and girls chose I Love Rock & Roll. They were surprised nobody has already sung that song, after all, the karaoke theme was rock & roll. They all were surprisingly good and the crowd was clearly enjoying their performances. Hayley was not afraid to get on that stage. She had so much fun in her dream so doing karaoke for real was not an issue anymore. She was happy her sisters were there and they could enjoy it together.

They came back to Hayley's right before midnight. The karaoke finished at nine thirty but there was 70s-themed dancing after that and they really wanted to stay. After a few Tequilla shots, the twins didn't care anymore whether Liam was a real vampire or not. They enjoyed his company and danced with him a few times, making Hayley jealous.

- I had so much fun - Hayley said - Thanks guys for coming over.

- Yeah, it was fun. - April agreed - We need to do it again next weekend. Liam, it was nice to meet you. Hope to see you again soon.

- It was nice to meet you too, ladies. See you next time.

Hayley waved her sisters goodbye and closed the door.

- It went quite well, don't you think, Liam?

- Yes I think it was OK. Much better than what I have experienced so far with others... But you didn't tell them everything, did you?

- No, they are not ready yet. We can tell them next week that you moved in and that we are engaged now. After that, I can tell them about my big decision. We need to spread the news over time, I can't just keep bombarding them with all this information. They have already taken a lot and thank god, they took it well.

- I think they got quite relaxed after that first round of shots.

- Yes – Hayley laughed – Tequilla took all the tension. You played your part quite well, by the way. You started talking to April about her paintings at the right moment. And karaoke was much better than staying home watching movies so thanks for coming up with that.

- I just wanted to help and I didn't want them to think I was a heartless monster. I'm glad it worked. It looks like you have nothing to worry about now, everything is fine and the way you wanted.

- You're right, I don't have to worry about anything. Everything is just perfect.

Next Saturday, Liam flew back to Illinois as his house sold that week and there was some paperwork he needed to take care of. All his stuff was already at Hayley's, delivered on Monday as planned. Three large suitcases of clothes and many carton boxes labelled 'books' started to pile at the driveway. Even though they were very heavy and delivery man struggled, Liam had no difficulties bringing everything into the house within just a couple of minutes, as if every box was full of feathers. They spent a nice evening on unpacking and going through the books. Although most of them were very old, they were still in perfect condition, with all pages holding together. Each book had a unique story of the place and time it was bought. Each reminded Liam of where he lived and who he met, that's why they were all so important and travelled with him from place to place, taking more and more room to store.

On Sunday, April and June were supposed to come after eleven o'clock like every other week. Hayley was anxious, looking for the right words, thinking how to bring the big news to the twins. She was walking between the kitchen and the living room, bringing more and more stuff to the table, completely unaware of what she was actually doing.

Lexi was watching her closely, following her around, hoping one of those deliciously smelling things would be for her. When Hayley heard the doorbell, she took a few deep breaths before she pressed the handle.

- Hi Hayley, I thought Liam would be here. – said April holding her painting wrapped in a brown protective paper.

- Unfortunately, he couldn't come.

- Oh, OK, I will leave the painting here for him to pick up. You were right, Hayley, he's very nice and easy to talk to. I still can't believe he's a vampire though. That sounds so weird and unreal.

- I know, but you'll get used to it.

They took their jackets off and sat comfortably on the sofas. Hayley's house was pleasantly warm and smelled of ginger and orange.

- So will you tell us now how you two met?

- Well… OK, let's try it…

Lexi lied down on the floor by the sofa, chewing on a big bone she's got from the twins. Hayley was pouring down the coffee, thinking intensively what to say. There was no easy way to explain how exactly she met Liam and trying to simplify that story could make it even more difficult to understand.

- Leah, the girl who wrote that journal, contacted me when I was in a hospital. She created a dream for me, when I was fighting for my life. In that dream, I met Liam. Although I was asleep for only two days, in my dream, a year passed by and during that time, I fell in love with Liam and we got engaged.

- Wow, sounds like a hell of a story. A year you say?

- Yes. Leah got into Liam's head too and created the same dream for him. I didn't know where to find Liam because in my dream, he lived here in Aspen but he knew where to look for me. So when he woke up, he came to Aspen to find me. And he did, obviously.

- So... you two met through a magically created dream, without knowing each other in real life?

- Correct.

- Wow. I would say it's unbelievable but recently, nothing seems to be impossible anymore.

- So, in real life, I have known Liam for about two weeks now. But technically, we have known each other for over a year. In that dream we both were exactly as we are in reality. What we thought and what we felt was real. Does this make any sense?

- Of course not! But we follow. - June said laughing.

- OK. Like I said, in our dream, we got to know each other pretty well and at some point, we got engaged. Now, that we are together for real, we decided to get back to where we have left off in the dream.

- So you're engaged, is that what you are trying to tell us?

- Well, yes.

- That sounds so messed up! Is there anything else you haven't told us yet? - April got a bit annoyed by the fact that Hayley waited that long to tell them about the engagement.

- That Liam has moved in here already.

April and June suddenly noticed the bookcase on the back wall. For some reason, they have not paid any attention to it earlier.

- I see his stuff is already here. - April said looking around the room.

- Hayley, are you sure about this? - June sounded concerned - Do you really know him?

- I already know more about him than anyone else ever. I don't expect you to understand this, you cannot possibly know what I went through when I was in that hospital. Leah knew me and she knew Liam too and she was sure that two of us were perfect for each other. And she was right, I love him very much and he loves me and we want to be together.

- But it looks like you didn't even know him before that dream.

- So? Every single pair of hearts started out as strangers.

- That's actually true.

- I heard it in a song.

They sat in silence, eating their pieces of cake. April and June liked Liam but they thought it was too early for Hayley to marry him. Although they were together for a year in the dream, they have only known each other for a few weeks in reality. But for Hayley it was completely different. She knew Liam inside out and she shared many amazing moments with him. She wanted to spend the whole eternity with him and she couldn't imagine any other scenario for her future.

- Girls, I need you to trust me. You know I have always been reasonable and down to earth. I know how it all sounds and that it's difficult to understand but I am sure this is a right decision and I really want to do this. I want to marry Liam and spend the rest of my life with him by my side. I am happy with him, I love spending time with him. When he leaves I feel sad, when he's away I can't wait to see him again.

- It sounds like love to me. - June smiled.

April and June started to understand that they could not stand in a way of Hayley's happiness. She has gone through a lot with her husband's death and attempted suicide. It looked like Liam was the key to Hayley's happiness and well-being and her sisters needed to be on her side, supporting her instead of getting in her way.

- Very well then. Congratulations, sister. I am happy for you.

- Me too. Congrats!

They got up and hugged and Lexi started jumping around and barking, trying to be a part of the happy circle.

- So, when is the wedding?

- We haven't decided yet.

- Would you like us to help you with the preparation or would you like us to stay away?

- Of course I would like you to help me. But to be honest with you, we don't want a big wedding. There will be only a few guests: you two, Liam's sister Isabella and her partner Ethan. I don't want anyone else to be there. I don't need any strangers to be a part of that special day.

- OK – June was thinking intensively – So do you have anything particular in mind? I don't think booking a whole restaurant for just six people is a good idea but we can't celebrate in a crowded bar or at home.

- Well… I was thinking… Maybe we could rent a boat, get married at sea and sail to Hawaii for our honeymoon.

- Sun, ocean, beach and lots of fun. I think it's a great idea, Hayley. We will organise everything, book the boat and the hotel so no need to worry about anything. So, when do you want to go?

- As soon as possible. Christmas is in two months and I would like to be back by then because I can't imagine Christmas wearing shorts and sunbathing. I need snow outside my window and biting cold that would chill me to the bone.

- Of course, let us check online and make some calls. If we can go there before Christmas we'll go, if not, we'll go in January. Either way, it's going to be perfect, I promise.

- I'm sure it will be. Thank you girls for your understanding, your opinion really means a lot to me. I love you two very much and I am so happy that I can be perfectly honest with you. I don't want to have any secrets and I don't want to lie to you and I know everything I've said recently is insane and hard to believe so I am really grateful that you decided to support me and join me, becoming a part of this amazing magical world.

- It's hard not to believe you when you see a man moving with a speed of light – said April with a smile – at first I really thought you were losing your mind and you really scared me but after meeting Liam, I breathed a sigh of relief. I freaked out a bit at first, I admit, but you trusted him and I trust you so if you say he's a good man then I believe you. I love you too very much and I am happy to see you happy, after all you've been through. And it doesn't really matter what I think and what my opinion is, the only thing that truly matters here is that you're happy so you can count on my full support and I will always be there for you and you don't need to lie to me or hide anything from me, afraid that I may disapprove.

- I'm one hundred percent with April – said June – whatever you need, I'm here. This is what family is for, to support each other.

Hayley smiled with tears in her eyes. As the words got stuck in her throat, she got up and hugged her sisters again, letting the tears of happiness run down her face.

Chapter 14

Weeks were slowly passing by as Hayley waited for a confirmation from her sisters regarding her wedding day. Even though every weekday and every weekend looked exactly the same, Hayley didn't complain. She spent every free moment with Liam watching movies, walking with Lexi and relaxing by the fireplace. They skied every Saturday and met with April and June every Sunday. Every week, the twins came over around eleven, stayed for lunch and dinner and all four went to karaoke and dancing after that. It never got boring and it was always fun. They enjoyed each other's company completely forgetting about magic and never talking about it. Even before the weeding, Liam was already a part of the family and Hayley was happy that she could spend time with her sisters and Liam without a need to choose one or another. Isabella and Ethan visited them once. In real life, these two have been together for a few decades now. The friendship between Isabella and Hayley was not as strong as in her dream, but they liked each other and enjoyed each other's company. Isabella was really a bounty hunter but not as cruel as Leah depicted her in Hayley's dream. There was no psychological torture involved and none of her bounties has ever found out that she was a vampire. When Hayley told Isabella about that part of her dream, they both had a good laugh.

The twins managed to get everything ready for the wedding before Christmas. They booked their flights from Aspen to Los Angeles for the first of December. They had a small yacht booked for two weeks and a hotel on the island for a week. A flight back home has been booked for twenty-third of December, so Hayley could have her white Christmas as she wished.

It was the first of December and everyone was already packed and ready for the trip. They had their flight at ten in the morning so they could board the yacht at one o'clock. They all got on the plane in their winter coats and boots and changed into polo shirts and trainers when landed in California. The captain was waiting for them in the Port of Long Beach. He was a very nice, middle-aged man with grey hair and a short grey beard.

- Hello everyone. I hope you had a nice flight. My name is Anthony Parker and I will be your captain. Welcome on board.

- Hello Anthony – April reached out her hand to greet him – Nice to meet you. My name is April, we've spoken over the phone.

The rest of the pack just waved to Anthony without introducing themselves. They knew he was not going to remember their names anyway. They boarded the *Grace* and found their rooms below deck. The yacht was for twelve people so they had plenty of space. It was a bit larger than the yacht Hayley remembered from her dream but it was equally fancy, elegant and comfortable. Three large sofas on the upper deck were decorated with soft navy pillows and each bedroom floor was covered with a thick, soft, fluffy navy carpet. The fridge was full of water bottles, fizzy drinks and alcohol but Hayley still managed to find a spot for a few blood bags for her vampire guests. There was one more smaller fridge that Hayley was forbidden to open as it stored the wedding cake. She was also forbidden to go to April's or June's room but the more they were saying 'stay away' the more Hayley was tempted to have a look. She felt like a small kid who knew her birthday presents were already bought and hidden somewhere by her parents and she needed to wait for a big day before she could open them.

It was twenty-one degrees Celsius and sunny. A very nice change from minus five that they had that morning in Aspen. The captain informed them that the weather was supposed to be nice for the whole journey so he planned on reaching Hawaiian port within two weeks as estimated by the twins.

That afternoon they all spent on the deck, talking, drinking and laughing. They all had many stories they wanted to share with the rest of the group. Hayley was cuddling up to Liam and looking at her friends having a good time. She was so happy it all turned out that way. She was so disappointed and sad when she woke up in that hospital a few months ago and now everything was going so well. She was ready to marry Liam and spend the rest of her life with him. She was also ready to turn into a vampire so she could live forever by his side. It was her last day as Mrs Evans. Tomorrow she would become Mrs Anderson and she couldn't wait to say 'I do'. She didn't expect a fancy ceremony and it didn't have to be her dream wedding, but she hoped that her life after that day would be her dream come true and she couldn't wait for it to begin.

The next day Liam woke Hayley up with his kisses.

- Good morning, you are going to be a bride today. Nervous?

- Not really. I'm glad it's only six of us here.

- Me too. I don't need a big ceremony in front of any strangers. It's going to be great.

- I know it is. I'm so happy to be here and I can't wait to meet Leah one day and thank her for what she's done for us. It's so unfair that she can communicate with us whenever she wants and we can't do the same. Leah, if you can hear me, thank you for your help. I wish you could be here with us.

- Stop talking to invisible people and get ready for your big day. Your sisters are already awake.

- Really? They're no early birds so I'm surprised they got out of the bed before nine. Let me see what they're up to.

Hayley got up and dressed for breakfast. She was amazed when she saw the whole deck decorated with flowers, ribbons and balloons. April and June must have spent the whole night to get that ready. They managed to change a simple yacht into a boat from a fairy tale. And even though the scent of roses and lilies faded on the open sea, their beauty continued to delight.

- So, do you like it? - asked April. Despite spending the whole night on the wedding preparations, she was full of energy and unusually hyperactive.

- I love it. It's beautiful, thank you. - Hayley kissed April on a cheek and put her arm around her. – How many cups of coffee have you had so far?

- Enough to keep me going for another twelve hours. Don't worry about me, I'm fine. Now, come with me.

April led Hayley to her room. June was already there, taking care of the bouquet. A small bouquet made of roses and gypsophila, carefully tied with a white ribbon, matched the decor on board.

- You said you didn't want a white dress, so we got you this.

April opened the closet and showed Hayley the dress. It was ivory, made of satin, with lace neckline and back and long lace sleeves. Hayley was looking at it with her jaw down.

- And? What do you think?

- I love it! - Hayley was deeply moved and tears came to her eyes - It's so beautiful, you must have spent a fortune on this.

- Don't worry, this is a present from all of us. We chipped in.

- Thank you so much!

Hayley trapped both her sisters at once in a very uncomfortable embrace.

- I'm glad you like it. But it's very delicate so be careful. By the way, what did you do with Lexi?

- My colleague took her. Our dogs already played together in the park a few times so they should get along just fine.

- We have completely forgotten about her when planning this trip.

- Don't worry, you have taken care of everything flawlessly and taking care of Lexi was the only thing that was on my list.

Liam and Ethan were enjoying the sun on the deck, drinking bourbon and playing cards when Hayley spent the rest of the day on preparing for the wedding. Boys wanted to help the girls with the preparation but they didn't let them do it.

- You won't do anything right and I will have to redo everything myself anyway, so don't touch anything and just go! - Isabella was very clear that she didn't want them anywhere near anything wedding-related.

She was taking care of the decorations with April while June was doing Hayley's makeup and hair.

- I can't believe you are getting married again and I don't even have a boyfriend.

- Don't worry June, you're only twenty, you still have plenty of time to find your mister right.

- I hope I'll find my Liam one day. Maybe Leah can show me some nice guy in my dream too.

They both laughed.

- I almost forgot! - June yelled and started nervously going through her suitcase.

She handed Hayley a pair of small diamond earrings.

- You needed something old and borrowed and I thought these would look lovely on you.

- Thank you June. That's so sweet. - Hayley put the earrings on.

- June… I know that we haven't had a chance to talk about it before and it all happened so fast… and I didn't want to flood you with information…

- What is it Hayley? You can tell me anything. After all these witches and vampires I don't think there is anything that can surprise me now.

- Would you still love me if I was like Liam?

June started to understand what Hayley was trying to say and it surprised her after all. She looked at Hayley, thinking intensively on how to respond.

- The truth is that… I don't even know what that truly means. I know about the speed and the eating habit… But what else would change? And why would you want this anyway?

- Because I'm in love and I want to be with Liam. But he won't grow old and I will. He will live forever and I would eventually die… I was turned in my dream and I remember what it felt like and I loved it. Nothing would change for you or April, I would still be your sister who loves you very much. And I would still visit. It will be all the same. That change is only for me and Liam.

- Did he ask you to do that?

- This is something that I wanted myself.

June thought for a minute before she replied. She still didn't quite understand what that meant. She was trying to put all the pieces of information together to get some clearer picture.

- Hayley, this is your life and you should do with it whatever feels right in your heart. I thought it would be selfish of Liam to expect this from you, but it would be selfish of me to expect you not to do this only because it scares me.

- Don't be scared June. Like I said you won't notice anything.

- So why are you telling me this? Looks like you didn't have to.

- Because I want to be honest with you. Because, when the time comes, I want you to know who I really am. Besides, with time, you'd probably notice something and I thought it's better to talk to you now rather than tiptoe around you all the time.

- I appreciate your honesty Hayley. Do what you think is best for you.

- Thank you, sister.

It was going to be a very emotional day and they both already had enough of crying but they couldn't stop their tears from falling.

The ceremony was planned to begin at sunset around five o'clock. Everything was prepared and everyone was ready on the deck. Hayley was standing in her room, looking into the mirror. Her hair and makeup were done, the dress fitted perfectly and she was about to cry again when April knocked on her door.

- Look at you… You look perfect!

- It's thanks to you and June. You two did a magnificent work with the make-up and the dress. It's not that much about me, you know.

April approached Hayley with a small box in her hand.

- You should have something new and blue so I got you this.

Hayley opened the box. It was a beautiful sapphire neckless.

- I thought it would match your engagement ring.

- It's beautiful thank you April. I love it. April… there is something I wanted to tell you. I thought about it a lot and... I decided I would like to be like Liam. Do you know what I mean?

April smiled.

- I know. If that's what you want then do it.

- You don't seem surprised.

- I expected you would say that eventually. It was kind of obvious or maybe I have just read too many books about vampires, but this decision makes sense to me.

- And are you OK with that?

- Why wouldn't I be? I expect you would stay the same, right? I mean… Liam is nice so I assume you won't change into some blood-thirsty monster.

- Nothing would change, I promise.

- So, are you ready?

Hayley took a look in the mirror one last time.

- I'm ready.

Exactly at sunset, everyone was waiting on the deck for the bride. April played Guardian by Lindsey Stirling on her phone and Hayley started slowly walking towards Liam. She promised herself she wouldn't cry but it was harder than she thought. She reached the small altar that June and April built especially for that occasion. It was decorated with small pink roses and white ribbons like the chairs the guest were sitting on. Liam looked perfect in his black suit, smiling from ear to ear.

April stopped the song and the captain started the ceremony.

- Dearly beloved, we have gathered here today to witness Hayley and Liam, as they exchange their vows of marriage…

They didn't prepare their own vows. At first, they wanted to but then Hayley realised that she would probably get all emotional and wouldn't be able to say a single sentence. They decided that it would be better to stick with the usual wedding ceremony and a simple 'I do' would be enough. They wanted to keep it nice and short.

- Do you Hayley Evans – the captain continued - take Liam to be your lawfully wedded husband, to love, to have and to hold, from this day forward, as long as you both shall live?

- I do. - Hayley said it quietly trying to fight the tears.

- Do you Liam Anderson take Hayley to be your lawfully wedded wife, to love, to have and to hold, from this day forward, as long as you both shall live?

- I do.

- Having openly declared yourselves in accordance with the laws of the State of California, before everyone here, I now pronounce you a husband and wife. You may kiss the bride.

The ceremony was perfect and very emotional. The sunset was beautiful and Hayley was so relieved it was not raining. They all sat down for a cake. It was small single-tier vanilla cake, beautifully decorated with real strawberries and white roses.

- I'd like to make a toast – Isabella got up with a glass of champagne in her hand - To the newly married couple. I wish you a lifetime of happiness. Cheers!

Before she sat down, April and June got up.

- We'd like to say a few words too – April started – Hayley, our dearest sister, we are so glad that happiness found you again. You deserve eternity of joy with a true love by your side.

- Liam, - June took over - we hope Hayley is everything you ever wanted and you two will bring each other happiness. Welcome to the family. To Hayley and Liam!

- I think I should say something too – Ethan got up from his seat – although I admit I didn't prepare for this. So I will just say shortly that I wish you all the best.

- Thank you Ethan. Thank you all for your kind words – said Liam - It means a lot to me and Hayley that you are here with us today, celebrating the beginning of this new chapter. Hayley, I am looking forward to living this life with you. I love you.

- I love you too. To all of us. Cheers!

Everyone had fun. Even the captain had a dance or two with the twins as the water was calm. The music was playing, the champaign was pouring, everyone was dancing and having a good time. The weather was perfect, the night sky was clear and lit up with stars. Although the temperature fell down now to only ten degrees Celsius, nobody seemed to be bothered. The dancing and the alcohol warmed them all up. The wedding finished around five in the morning, when the sun was still down and the moon could still be seen in the sky. April and June were half-alive after another sleepless night. Hayley was also feeling tired but the rest of the group didn't show any signs of fatigue. Hayley put her beautiful wedding dress back to the closet and started to remove her make-up.

- I had a really good time today.

- Was it like you imagined it? - asked Liam.

- It was perfect. April and June did a wonderful job with the decorations. And this dress... It's more than I hoped for.

- I'm happy that you're happy.

- And are you happy for yourself?

- Do you really need to ask me that question, Hayley? Of course I am happy. I have just married the love of my life. The one and only. The girl who just made a vow to be with me forever.

- Yes, about that... I will turn when I'm back home. I need a witch to do the spell so I don't hurt anyone.

- Whenever you feel ready. No pressure.

- Thank you Liam... I am just wondering though...

- Tell me.

- Will you still love me the same after I turn?

- Of course I will. How can you doubt that?

- You know… now you think that you may lose me anytime, that I may die and any day spent together might be our last. Will you still feel the same about me knowing that I will live forever?

- Hayley, I love you and I always will no matter what you decide. And if you had to ask me that question you obviously don't know how much you mean to me and how much I care about you.

- I think I am just insecure, that's all.

- Don't be, you have nothing to worry about. You had a perfect day today and let's keep it that way. No worries, no tears, no troubles. You have an amazing future ahead of you, focus on that.

The next two weeks they have spent on the yacht, sailing towards Honolulu harbour. Every now and then, the captain stopped so they could swim in the ocean. The weather has been perfect so far and they hoped it would stay that way. But the last twenty-four hours didn't look that promising. The sky got grey, covered with heavy clouds and it started to rain. The ocean became restless and the waves got bigger. The captain was doing his best trying to keep them all safe but the weather was getting worse by the minute. Everyone was below deck with their life jackets on, preparing for the worst.

- I can't stand this anymore – April started to panic.

- Everything is going to be OK. – June said although she didn't sound convincing when her own voice was shaking - Our captain is very experienced and he knows what to do.

But April was panicking more and more. Her heart was beating fast and she started feeling dizzy and sick.

- I need this to stop… I can't stand it anymore…

Everyone was anxious but for some reason April was the most terrified of them all. Her wide-open eyes were full of tears and she struggled to catch her breath.

- April, calm down…

- Enough! - April yelled furiously.

In that moment, everything changed. The ocean got calmer, the waves got smaller, the rain stopped and the yacht was now just rocking gently like a cradle. They all looked at April shocked but she was surprised too.

- How did you do it? – asked Hayley surprised.

- I didn't do anything.

- The storm ended because of you. This cannot be a coincidence.

- That's impossible. I didn't do anything.

- So, now we know that April's a witch – said Liam with a gentle smile, not being surprised at all.

- So if I really am a witch – April said – how come I didn't know that?

- Because you never practised it. You never used it until now.

- But why now?

- I think it's because you were angry and afraid. You wanted the storm to stop and so it did.

- Don't worry April – Hayley said with a smile trying to calm her sister down – once we're back home, we will meet with Sarah, my witch friend who will be able to help you.

- Worry? – asked April furrowing her brow - I am not worried, Hayley. I'm a witch! How cool is that? I can't wait to see what I am capable of. That was amazing! I wish you could feel that power.

- So, are you OK?

- Sure I am! I'm great! I wish I've discovered that earlier. All these years I've wasted when I could learn and practice magic. Why didn't Leah tell me anything by entering my dreams? I will never forgive her that.

- Don't be angry with Leah, maybe you were not ready yet and she knew about it, maybe it's better that you discovered it yourself. Leah was just a teenager when she found out and it scared her a lot so I think it's good it happened now and not earlier. Now, try not to get too angry or too frightened so we don't see what else you can do. You're going to Hawaii so you're supposed to be relaxed and have a good time. Focus on that for now and when we're back home you'll meet with Sarah and she will be able to guide you.

- I will behave, I promise Hayley. I won't do anything to ruin your honeymoon, you have my word. Now, let's go back to beds, I'm guessing it will be nothing but a smooth sailing from now on. I'll make sure of it – she added with a smile.

One week on the island was exactly as Hayley imagined it. Jet ski, horse riding, dancing in the moonlight and karaoke. They enjoyed the last few days of warmth and sun before they needed to come back to freezing and covered in snow Aspen.

Hayley was lying on the beach, looking at the ocean and the setting sun. It was shortly after five o'clock but the beach was still quite busy. Obviously, nobody wanted to waste their time on being in a hotel.

- If I were already a vampire, what would be different? I mean here, now, on this beach.

Liam had a look around.

- On your left, do you see those two kids playing in the sand? One of them is wearing incredibly bright orange shorts.

Hayley nodded.

- You would hear their laughter. You would also hear their mother telling them not to eat the sand.

- Are you serious? They're so far away! And you can hear them? Despite all this noise around? Despite the sound of the ocean?

- Yes. I can also see a nice shell partially covered by the sand right over there – although he pointed it to Hayley, she couldn't see it - I think you would like it. Maybe you'd like to take it home as a souvenir. It would be more valuable than something bought in a shop.

- Then go and bring it to me.

Liam got up and ran about twenty meters.

- I love you – whispered Hayley when Liam was picking up the shell.

- I heard that! – he yelled back.

'Unbelievable' – thought Hayley – *'Even with all my senses working fine, I am still missing out. I can't wait to see the world the way he sees it, to experience the surrounding the way he does. It's like he lives in a whole new world, beyond the world I live in now.'*

- This is for you – said Liam handing the shell to Hayley.

It was in several colours. The top was in a few pink shades and the rest of the shell was covered in uneven orange and yellow stripes and a few white spots.

- A sunrise shell – said Hayley with a smile. – it is beautiful, thank you Liam.

- So, is your time in Hawaii as good as it was in your dream?

- It's even better because this time, it is for real. *'Or at least I hope it is.'*

Chapter 15

The next day after flying back from Hawaii, Hayley started decorating her house for Christmas. She was putting up the tree with Christmas songs playing in the background. Liam wanted to help but Hayley didn't let him. Decorating the house was what she waited for the entire year and it always brought her so much joy. When Hayley was at home, Liam was out buying their Christmas dinner. There was no time to cook so everything had to be ordered. To avoid any disappointments, they decided to do Secret Santa along with the wish list. Everyone said exactly what they wanted and all presents were bought in November, before their trip to Hawaii.

At six o'clock, everything was ready. The dinner was on the table, the Christmas tree was decorated, presents were lying underneath and everyone has already arrived. The tree looked beautiful, decorated with baubles in red, gold and silver and even though it was artificial, nobody could tell as the quality was worth its incredibly high price. But Hayley loved Christmas time very much and she was ready to spend every cent on it just to make sure everything was perfect. The table was bending under the turkey, yams, stuffing and baked ham. The frost outside naturally decorated the windows, creating extraordinary shapes on the glass and a thick layer of snow covering the front and the back of the house was reflecting the moonlight, sparkling like diamonds.

Everyone ate to their hearts' content and yet, there was still plenty of turkey left. They were sitting in the living room, drinking wine and breathing heavily, unable to even look at any more food. Lexi was lying by the fireplace chewing the bone. Hayley looked at her friends and family and raised her glass.

- I just wanted to say that I am really grateful for you all being here with me today. Christmas time felt always so magical but I have never thought of having Christmas dinner with vampires and witches. I assume this year's Christmas was as magical as it could get so thank you all for making this special time even more special for me. Cheers!

They all raised their glasses and made a toast. Christmas that year was special indeed. Three vampires, two humans, a witch and a dog under one roof. Hayley was right, that Christmas couldn't get any more magical and it was more than she ever hoped for. It was good to have a house full of laughter again, with everyone she loved and cared about right there in one room.

- Come on everyone, time for a photo!

- Don't make me move – said April sitting on the floor with her back leaned against the sofa where barely alive June was lying and breathing heavily.

Hayley brought the tripod and set the self-timer for ten seconds. She sat quickly on the rug, squeezing between Liam and April

- Say cheese! – she yelled right before the camera lamp flashed.

On the thirty-first of December they were all packing for their plane to Louisiana as they all decided to spend the New Year's Eve in New Orleans. Having spoken with Sarah, April decided to go there to practice her magic so they thought it would be a good idea to fly there with her. According to Sarah, there was no better place for a witch than a French Quarter in the Crescent City and the local witches would make excellent tutors.

Hayley was all packed now and waited for Liam to come back home. He was dropping Lexi off to Aspen Valley

Kennel as there was nobody else to take care of her on New Year's Eve. While sitting alone at home, Hayley took her diary out of the wardrobe and started writing:

'Another year has passed by. I am sitting and reminiscing about what has happened during these three hundred and sixty-five days. I started this year with tears of sorrow in my eyes. I was lonely and depressed and saw no future ahead. Then, I nearly died and came back to life completely changed. Now, I am able to find brief moments of happiness every day. Lexi turned my world upside down and brought me so much joy, April and June became my best friends and Liam gave my life meaning. I discovered vivid colours of real magic in this black and white world and I cannot wait to become a real part of it. I decided I will end my human existence and start my new life on first of January. I will celebrate my new self in New Orleans, the most magical place on earth. My life is going in a good direction and I am genuinely happy now. I guess, in the end, it doesn't really matter what you own or what you achieved, it's the people that truly matter – love, friendship and family. Now I have it all and I am looking forward to living my eternal life, appreciating every moment I spend with those I care about the most. I'm ready to leave the past behind. I'm ready for a new beginning.'

Shortly after ten in the morning, they all arrived at Monteleone Hotel, the most prestigious hotel in New Orleans. The New Year's Eve party was starting at nine in the evening so they still had plenty of time to kill.

- Liam, I wanted to tell you something. – said Hayley as they were unpacking in their room.

- What is it Hayley?

- I decided I want you to turn me at midnight.

- And how do you want to do this, exactly?

- I will leave this with you to decide. Figure something out, I can't think about it. I just want this to be quick and painless.

- OK… As weird as it sounds, you can count on me.

They had a four-hour trip planned to visit French Quarter, Garden District and the cemetery. It was fifteen degrees Celsius and sunny and the streets were slowly getting crowded as everyone was coming over for New Year's Eve. After two o'clock, they all went to Galatoire's for lunch. It was a very fancy and elegant restaurant but it was conveniently situated on Bourbon Street, two minutes away from their hotel.

- So, how did you like the tour? - Hayley started the conversation.

- Well.. it was quite interesting. - April said - But now when I know it's not just a tourist attraction…

- Yes, about that – June interrupted – so if I go to one of those fortune-tellers, will they be truly able to tell me my future?

- I don't know – April said – I am meeting Iris in forty minutes so you can ask her. She will be the one helping me. Sarah recommended her to me.

- Would that be OK if we stayed for a few minutes? - Hayley asked. – to see who you'll be dealing with?

- Yes, I think so. But I will leave it for Iris to decide.

Iris came over shortly before three o'clock. She looked quite ordinary. In contrary to Sarah, she didn't have many rings or bracelets, but only one silver ring with an onyx stone and matching necklace. Her eyes were incredibly green with golden circles around her pupils. She was in her forties, slim and tall and her long brown hair fell loosely down her back to the waistline. She approached the table without a second of hesitation, as if she knew them all already or as if they stood out in the crowded restaurant.

- April, hi, I'm Iris.

- Hi Iris, thank you for meeting me. These are my friends. They wanted to meet you if you don't mind.

- Not at all. I see some of them are quite extraordinary. It's nothing unusual to see their kind here in New Orleans, but I didn't expect them to be your company.

- They are part on my family now. Liam is my brother-in-law.

- Interesting…

- So Iris – Hayley joined the conversation – what are you going to teach my little sister?

- Well, I will introduce a few simple spells so she can start using her magic in a more controlled way. I will also teach her to talk to our ancestors so she can talk to Leah.

Hayley took Leah's ring off her finger..

- Are you able to create another one like this?

Iris took the ring and looked at it carefully.

- This is a very powerful spell.

- I know. But since you'll be talking to Leah, maybe she can tell you how she made it. I would like my sisters to have this ring but as you can see I have two sisters and only one magical ring.

- Don't you want one more for yourself?

Hayley hesitated with an answer. She didn't want Iris to know what future she has already planned for herself.

- I'm fine.

- Very well. I'll see what I can do.

Iris handed the ring to April.

- For safekeeping, better you have it. It's your family heirloom after all.

- Thank you. June, I will do my best to get another one for you too.

- Thank you sister. Iris, I have a question – June began uncertainly – Is there any real fortune-teller in New Orleans?

Even though she was surrounded by vampires and witches, June still felt silly asking that question, like a small child asking grown-ups whether Santa Claus was real.

- Yes, there are a few real witches performing. They can tell you what people or places to avoid or what your future husband may look like or how many kids you may have but nothing concrete. You will not find out how long you will live or whether your future is full of joy or sorrow.

- Who to talk to about that husband and kids thing?

- Look for Heather. She works at Hex Old World Witchery on Decatur Street.

- Thanks Iris.

- It's time for us go now – Liam got up. - We have a river cruise planned this afternoon. It was nice to meet you Iris. Happy New Year.

- Thank you. Happy New Year to you too.

They got up and went for their river cruise, leaving April and Iris in the restaurant. They still had a few more hours till sunset and sitting in a restaurant felt like a waste of time. The city was beautiful and they wanted to see as much of it as possible. The streets were decorated for the celebration and were getting more and more crowded. Despite an early hour, many people were already quite drunk and were most likely to miss the midnight. It was very loud and noisy as different music was pouring from all directions, people were screaming and laughing and it was nearly impossible to stay focused and gather some thoughts. But everyone enjoyed the atmosphere, nonetheless. After all, there was a reason for celebration and the New Year should not begin in silence and solitude.

After their cruise, June, Hayley and Isabella went to see Heather. Liam and Ethan went to the bar nearby to drink some bourbon and listen to jazz. They were not interested in witchcraft and the fortune telling. The store was quite dark, full of voodoo dolls, potions, books and candles and the smell of herbs was very intense. The girl who approached them was far from ordinary. She wore a loose dress like a hippie and her brown wavy hair was pinned up high on her head in a large bun. She had lots of silver bracelets that jingled with every slightest movement of her hand.

- Hello ladies, how can I help you? What are you looking for?

- We're here to see Heather.

- Sure. I will let her know. Wait here.

The girl came back in a minute with a tall dark-haired woman with incredibly amber eyes. She looked more like Iris wearing a simple white t-shirt and jeans which was a bit disappointing as the girls expected a fortune teller would look more witchy maybe even mysterious.

- Hi Heather – June started – Iris recommended you to us.

- Are you friends of Iris'?

- I wouldn't say 'friends'. We met her earlier today, she will be teaching my sister.

- I understand. Follow me.

June went first. She followed Heather to a small room with two chairs and a small round table. There was some incense burning at the back, smelling like a cinnamon.

- June, you know I cannot tell you any details, nothing specific, just a general image.

- I know, Iris explained that to me. I just want to know whether I would ever get married and have any kids.

- I can tell you that.

Heather took June's hand and closed her eyes. She was deep in thought, not saying anything. After a couple of minutes she opened her eyes and looked at June with a gentle smile.

- You will have a beautiful family June. I see a handsome man and two little blonde twin girls.

June smiled.

- That's sounds great, thank you Heather. I don't need to know anything more, that's all I wanted to know. Happy New Year.

- You too June. Wish you lots of happiness. Please, have a look around our store. Maybe you'll find something suitable for yourself. Does any of you two have any questions for me? – she added looking at Isabella and Hayley.

- Not really – Isabella answered – I just wanted to get a nice ring or a bracelet.

- Yes, well, I don't think I have enough time to talk to you about your eternity anyway. There's plenty ahead of you, that's for sure.

Isabella smiled. She was not interested in knowing her future, she was happy with her life as it was so whatever was coming next she was ready to face it and accept it.

- How about you? – she asked looking at Hayley.

- I already got married and I am sure there will be no more weddings in my life. I don't plan to have any kids either so I don't think there is anything you can tell me.

Heather approached Hayley and took her hand but quickly took a step back, with her face serious and her brow furrowed.

- Are you sure you know what you are doing?

It was obvious she knew what Hayley has planned for herself.

- Yes, this is exactly what I want.

- Very well, I cannot tell you what's best for you. As long as you know what you're getting yourself into, that's all that matters to me. I don't want you to be talked into this and fed misinformation.

- You don't need to worry about me. I know exactly what I'm doing. Nice meeting you Heather. Happy New Year.

The girls left the store with some jewellery and candles. June was happy knowing that her future was bright and promising. She just wished she knew how much longer she needed to wait for that future to become her reality but

Heather was not allowed to tell her that. She needed to wait patiently for what's yet to come although it was very tempting to go back there and offer the witch enough money to make her break some rules and give June more details. Even though she was sure the witch wouldn't accept her offer, she spent the rest of the day wondering what if.

The party started at nine o'clock sharp when the air was filled with anticipation. The club was very crowded, but everyone managed to find themselves a nice spot on the dance floor. It was completely different from all the other parties they had attended that year—no karaoke, no themed playlists, just a DJ and a crowded dancefloor. The colourful lighting shifted in time with the music creating shadows dancing on the walls. The room was loud, with bass reverberating through their chests. There was a sense of joy and freedom in the air and undeniably everyone had a good time. DJ kept the energy high, engaging the crowd with asking everyone to jump, wave their hands in the air, or clap along to the beats. Every so often, the music would pause, and the DJ would encourage the crowd to continue singing a cappella. It was a night of pure fun, full of vibrant energy that seemed endless.

. Right before midnight, they all left the club and started walking towards Mississippi river for the fireworks display.

- Guys, if you don't mind we'll go to the hotel now and watch the fireworks from the roof. - Hayley tried to sound convincing.

- No worries. We'll see you next year then – April smiled and gave Hayley a hug – Happy New Year sister.

- Happy New Year April.

Liam took Hayley's hand and they started walking back to the hotel. The night was cold but not freezing like in Aspen at that time of the year. The sky was a bit cloudy but it was not raining so everyone was looking forward to the fireworks display at midnight. Many people were going to the river, passing by Hayley and Liam, wishing them a

Happy New Year or looking at them surprised, wondering why they were going in the opposite direction.

- You'll miss the fireworks – said Liam as they were going up the stairs to their hotel room. – would you like to wait a few more minutes?

- No, I want this done at midnight. I've seen fireworks before, I can live with missing them this one time.

They went inside the room, locked the door and covered all windows. They didn't want anyone to witness what was about to happen.

- So, did you decide how you want to do it? - Hayley asked. She sounded nervous but excited.

- Yes.

- And?

- I won't tell you.

- Why not?

- Because I don't want you to think too much about it. You won't feel anything, you have my word.

- Fair enough. Shouldn't I drink your blood or something?

- That's already done. I added a few drops to your drink at the restaurant. You didn't even know.

They heard the crowd outside counting down.

- *Eleven, ten...*

- Are you sure about this? – Liam asked one last time, standing in front of Hayley and putting his hands around her neck.

- *Eight, seven...*

- Absolutely. I love you.

- *Six, five...*

- I love you too. Happy New Year.

- *Three, two, one...*